MW01129432

Protected

The Queen's Alpha Series, Volume 8

W.J. May

Published by Dark Shadow Publishing, 2018.

This is a work of fiction. Similarities to real people, places, or events are entirely coincidental.

PROTECTED

First edition. November 15, 2018.

Copyright © 2018 W.J. May.

Written by W.J. May.

Also by W.J. May

Bit-Lit Series
Lost Vampire
Cost of Blood
Price of Death

Blood Red Series
Courage Runs Red
The Night Watch
Marked by Courage
Forever Night

Daughters of Darkness: Victoria's Journey
Victoria
Huntress
Coveted (A Vampire & Paranormal Romance)
Twisted
Daughter of Darkness - Victoria - Box Set

Hidden Secrets Saga
Seventh Mark - Part 1
Seventh Mark - Part 2
Marked By Destiny
Compelled
Fate's Intervention
Chosen Three
The Hidden Secrets Saga: The Complete Series

Kerrigan Chronicles
Stopping Time
A Passage of Time
Ticking Clock

Mending Magic Series
Lost Souls

Paranormal Huntress Series
Never Look Back
Coven Master
Alpha's Permission
Blood Bonding
Oracle of Nightmares
Shadows in the Night
Paranormal Huntress BOX SET #1-3

Christmas Before the Magic
Question the Darkness
Into the Darkness
Fight the Darkness
Alone in the Darkness
Lost in Darkness
The Chronicles of Kerrigan Prequel Series Books #1-3

The Chronicles of Kerrigan Sequel
A Matter of Time
Time Piece
Second Chance
Glitch in Time
Our Time
Precious Time

The Hidden Secrets Saga
Seventh Mark (part 1 & 2)

The Queen's Alpha Series
Eternal
Everlasting
Unceasing
Evermore
Forever
Boundless
Prophecy
Protected

The Senseless Series
Radium Halos
Radium Halos - Part 2
Nonsense

Standalone
Shadow of Doubt (Part 1 & 2)
Five Shades of Fantasy
Shadow of Doubt - Part 1
Shadow of Doubt - Part 2
Four and a Half Shades of Fantasy
Dream Fighter
What Creeps in the Night
Forest of the Forbidden
Arcane Forest: A Fantasy Anthology
The First Fantasy Box Set

Watch for more at https://www.facebook.com/USA-TODAY-Best-seller-WJ-May-Author-141170442608149/.

THE QUEEN'S ALPHA SERIES
PROTECTED

USA TODAY BESTSELLING AUTHOR
W. J. MAY

Copyright 2018 by W.J. May

Have You Read the C.o.K Series?

The Chronicles of Kerrigan

Book I - *Rae of Hope* is FREE!

BOOK TRAILER:

http://www.youtube.com/watch?v=gILAwXxx8MU

How hard do you have to shake the family tree to find the truth about the past?

Fifteen year-old Rae Kerrigan never really knew her family's history. Her mother and father died when she was young and it is only when she accepts a scholarship to the prestigious Guilder Boarding School in England that a mysterious family secret is revealed.

Will the sins of the father be the sins of the daughter?

As Rae struggles with new friends, a new school and a star-struck forbidden love, she must also face the ultimate challenge: receive a tattoo on her sixteenth birthday with specific powers that may bind her to an unspeakable darkness. It's up to Rae to undo the dark evil in her family's past and have a ray of hope for her future.

Find W.J. May

Website:
http://www.wanitamay.yolasite.com
Facebook:
https://www.facebook.com/pages/Author-WJ-May-FAN-PAGE/
141170442608149
Newsletter:
SIGN UP FOR W.J. May's Newsletter to find out about new releases, updates, cover reveals and even freebies!
http://eepurl.com/97aYf

Prophecy Blurb:

USA Today Bestselling author, W.J. May, continues the highly antici-pated bestselling YA/NA series about love, betrayal, magic and fan-tasy. Be prepared to fight, it's the only option.

I will fight to the death for those I love.

What if you could freeze a moment in time?

Katerina Damaris thought her problems were finally over when she took her rightful place on the throne. But she had no idea of the trou-ble that was waiting when she got there.

When a mysterious curse freezes the palace and everyone inside, the young queen and her friends find themselves in a race against time to find out who's behind it. With the words of an ancient prophecy as their guide, they set out on a journey that will either end in the salva-tion of the realm or the destruction of everything they hold dear.

Old enemies resurface. Everyone's a target. And an ancient dark-ness is creeping over the land.

Is there a way to fight back the dark magic? Can Katerina unlock the secrets of the prophecy in time? Or have they learned that age-old lesson too late?

Some curses should never be broken...

Be careful who you trust. Even the devil was once an angel.

The Queen's Alpha Series

Eternal
Everlasting
Unceasing
Evermore
Forever
Boundless
Prophecy
Protected
Foretelling
Revelation
Betrayal
Resolved

Chapter 1

C*RASH!*
     The seven friends all stared at each other, then stared at the ceiling again. There wasn't a whisper of sound throughout the castle. Not a single breath. Just a dead, ringing silence punctured with the sporadic—

CRASH!

"What do you want to do?"

Old habits die hard. They hadn't been on the road together in months. They hadn't been sleeping in the wild, looking over their shoulders, or trying to outrun the constant danger at their backs. And yet, from the second they heard that first impact, every pair of eyes turned the same way.

"Dylan, what do you want to do?" Tanya asked again.

Normally, she might have asked her own boyfriend such a question. But Cassiel was frozen with a look of quiet dread—one foot angled subconsciously towards the main gate, as if he was dying to run away and leave it all behind him.

He had also recently been chewed on by a giant wolf.

"Dylan."

It was Aidan this time, less patient than Tanya.

In the beginning it hadn't been easy for him to surrender such decisions to the ranger, but he turned without hesitation now. The King of Belaria had long ago proven himself, and this certainly seemed like the kind of apocalyptic calamity that required his particular brand of skills.

"Yeah, I...just give me a second." Dylan's nose was still broken. He was still dripping wet from the river. And he'd recently resurrected his best friend from the dead. Dylan was dealing with quite enough at the moment without adding on an enchanted castle full of frozen people he used to know. Not to mention the ominous banging coming from up the stairs.

But his girlfriend was watching. And there were lives at stake.

With the kind of resilience that could only have come at a devastating price, he squared his shoulders and pulled in a jerking breath. "Okay, I'll check it out—"

A chorus of voices shouted him down, none louder than the vampire.

"Not what I meant!"

There was another crash. This one shook the very foundations of the castle.

"Need I remind you that, while you're gifted with all the supernatural qualities of a glorified St. Bernard, your girlfriend turns into an actual *dragon*?" Katerina's eyes flickered up to the ceiling with a thrill of anticipation. "If anyone's going after this thing, it's going to be me."

"Oh yeah?" A muscle twitched in the back of Dylan's jaw. Not once did he take his eyes off the grand staircase in the center of the hall. "That's a brave sentiment, sweetheart, but it makes me wonder if you've ever actually *seen* yourself as a dragon. You can't exactly play indoors."

"I'll go," Kailas volunteered quietly. "Of everyone here, I'm definitely the most—"

"Kailas, if you're about to say *expendable* I'll kill you myself," Katerina hissed.

Tanya hit him upside the head.

"Then what?" That famous calm of Dylan's had stretched as thin as it could go. "You think I'm going to let any of you do it? We have no idea what's up there—"

"All the more reason to stick together," Serafina interrupted. Even though she had woken up only seconds before, blinking slowly at a dandelion-haired pixie floating in the air above her head, she had recovered her wits quickly. A lot quicker than her older brother.

"Cass?"

As always, Dylan waited for a final opinion from his best friend. Looking for guidance, reassurance, the eternal balance to his whimsical disregard. But the fae had lost a part of himself the second they set foot in the castle. Between that and the fact that he'd only just returned to the land of the living, that 'eternal balance' was slightly skewed.

He didn't answer. Or maybe he couldn't. He simply forced his head up and down.

Yes. They would go together.

"All right," Dylan breathed, reaching back to take Katerina's hand. "Keep a tight formation, no one falls behind. The last thing we want is to... the last thing we want..."

The hint of a frown flickered through those blue eyes as he glanced over his shoulder.

"Did you guys just—"

CRASH!

It was impossible to know who screamed first. Katerina's ears were ringing with it, her throat was instantly raw. One second they were just standing there. The next, the doors of the castle had been ripped clear off the wall and inside charged a creature that could only be—

A CAVE TROLL?!

Katerina didn't think such a thing existed. After leaving her home she'd come to discover that some of the things from her 'fairytale' stories were real, and some weren't. Before they'd started dating Dylan had expressed a keen interest in meeting a mermaid, yet when she asked about the prospect of werewolves he had laughed in her face.

She'd thought cave trolls fell firmly into the category of those fictional characters. Judging by the looks on her friends' faces, they'd clearly thought so, too.

They were wrong. The screaming didn't stop.

"RUN!"

They had been programmed to fight. All of them had been pro-grammed to fight. But there was no fighting something like this. The only option was to escape.

"RUN!" Dylan shouted again.

He grabbed hold of Katerina's sleeve as they sprinted for the stairs, but before they'd made it even two steps the troll charged forward and the force of it knocked them off their feet. The tile floor rippled like water beneath them as he went rolling one way, and she went tumbling another.

The room blinked in and out of focus. Something warm was drip-ping down the back of her neck. Katerina lifted a dazed hand to her forehead, blinking heavily, then squinted in confusion as her eyes tried to make sense of what they were seeing.

This wasn't something you could fight, and yet... Cassiel was fight-ing it.

There was no explaining it. No way to reconcile the scene, and no way to ever forget. Even as she lay there, dazed and barely breathing, Katerina knew she'd remember the image as long as she lived. One man standing against a prehistoric giant. Facing down the monster without a hint of fear.

...Seven hells.

She'd seen Cassiel fight. He'd been the first one to help train her. She remembered being truly dazzled by the way he moved. Graceful as a dance. Fluid as water. Each movement delivering a swift yet strangely exquisite death. She knew now they had barely scratched the surface.

Because this? She had never seen anything like this.

"Cass—no!"

Serafina's cries fell on deaf ears. Her brother was in an entirely different world. One which didn't seem to uphold the basic laws of physics. Or gravity.

The troll's fist smashed down on the tile, but Cassiel was no longer there. Its hands flailed out wildly, but the fae had vanished. Every time

Katerina thought that tragedy had struck, that one of her dearest friends had just died right in front of her eyes, he would miraculously reappear.

How is this possible?

Katerina's jaw hit the floor as he sprinted straight up the castle wall—only to come down with devastating force upon the beast's head. He didn't have any weapons. None of them had any weapons. But it didn't seem to matter. As superfluous as it was absurd, the troll had brought a club. And Cassiel was more than happy to share.

Using the weight of his body as a lever, he grabbed the spiked end and leapt into the open air—flipping over twice before landing softly upon the floor. The club slipped out of the monster's hand. It landed with a deafening bang on the shattered tile, and while it was too heavy to lift the entire length of it was serrated, and the beast was already off balance. Two arrows fired into the side of its head and it stumbled to its knees, landing right on top of the giant spikes.

The scream that followed was so loud it shattered Katerina's ears. Dark gushes of blood rolled across the floor like a grisly tide. The beast tore itself free and tried to shriek again, but the second it threw back its head a sword lodged itself in the roof of its mouth.

Two spears were soon to follow.

Wait—arrows, swords, spears?

The young queen pushed weakly onto her elbows, vaguely aware that a bone was angled incorrectly in her wrist, only to realize what was happening. Cassiel hadn't been flying around aimlessly, rocketing off the walls like some sort of deadly angel. He had been travelling from person to frozen person—arming himself with each of their blades.

"Dylan!" He tossed his friend a knife, taken from her very own Hastings. The ranger had struck his head on a pile of rubble and was blinking at the fae in a similar daze. "Get up!"

The blade clattered across the floor, skidding to a stop just inches away from his hand. He stared at it for a moment, then lifted his eyes back to where his friend was fighting some sort of mythological brute. The next second he was racing forward to help, the knife clutched in his hand.

Together, they fought the beast back. Parrying back and forth, darting in and out with a synchronized skill that could only come from years of bloodshed and practice. One would attack, the other would defend. One would dive low, the other would jump high. They worked not to defeat, only to contain. Their friends were still lying on the floor—easy targets.

"Aidan!" Cassiel dropped suddenly to the ground, somersaulting to avoid the giant troll's outstretched hand. The tip of its claws raked the back of his neck, but he still managed to fire off an arrow before leaping back to his feet. "Stop skulking in the shadows and help!"

Skulking in the shadows actually translated to *fighting for his life.*

Aidan had been thrown under a stone balcony when the troll came in—a balcony which had promptly collapsed right on top of his head. He had been fighting to free himself ever since and had only just emerged, battered and bleeding, when he heard the fae's call. Slowly his eyes lifted to the monster they were fighting. He froze for a split second, then took a step away.

Vampires were creatures of instinct. They didn't enter a fight unless they sincerely believed that they could win. It said a lot that Aidan was visibly hesitating now.

Then the beast charged forward and he made up his mind.

"Tanya!"

The shape-shifter was still unconscious, but the troll was headed straight for her. She had time enough only to open her eyes, blink, then let out a terrified scream before its massive fist smashed into the tile where she had been lying. Except... she was no longer there.

The fae and the ranger might have been quick, but they didn't compare to the vampire.

Faster than sight Aidan snatched the tiny girl off the floor, spiriting her up the stairs just as the ground beneath them gave way. It was too fast for Katerina's eyes to follow. Just the memory of a shadow, and then he was gone. By the time she was able to find him again, Tanya had been deposited safely out of reach and he was flying back into the fight—fangs bared.

Only this time, he wasn't alone.

"Katerina—NO!"

Dylan actually turned his eyes away from the beast for a split second. Long enough to cast his girlfriend a stricken look as she charged into the battle. Long enough to have lost his leg if the vampire hadn't shoved him out of the way. He was still picking himself up off the floor when she charged past him—waves of liquid fire dripping from her hands.

"I was afraid of that," he muttered, scrambling to his feet.

The others didn't notice, as they were busy with the troll.

"Look out!" she called.

Cassiel, who had just buried a knife in the creature's neck, jumped free. Aidan, who had lodged a spear between its ribs, did the same. Yet neither one of them could manage to distance themselves far enough before the fire engulfed them like a cloud.

"KAT!" Dylan tackled her to the floor, wincing against the heat as the flames spluttered out in surprise. "It's tied to your emotions! Am I the only one who remembers you burning half the royal army to the ground? *And* the mountain they were standing on? Do NOT do it inside!"

"No—DO IT!"

They looked up at the same time to see both the vampire and the fae stumbling towards them. Their faces were smeared with soot and half their clothing was still on fire, but both were pointing excitedly behind them. The cave troll had dropped to one knee, screaming in pain and fury at the giant burns lacing up the side of its face.

"Do it again!" Cassiel commanded, throwing off his flaming cloak. "Only this time—"

A wave of fire blasted just inches above his head.

"For bloody sake! *Aim*, princess!"

Only Cassiel could manage to be condescending at a time like this. But the fire had done the trick. The beast was on the ropes. All that was left to do was finish it.

But how?

If anything, injuring the creature had only made it more dangerous. Its limbs thrashed out with no warning. Each violent motion cracking through iron and stone. Every time one of the friends tried to get close, they would end up leaping back. Every time they hurled another weapon, the beast would inadvertently swat it away. After several minutes of trying they quickly backed out of reach, gazing up at the monster in both exhaustion and fear.

"It's going to collapse the ceiling," Dylan murmured under his breath.

Katerina followed his gaze to the high rafters, then down to the various people still frozen about the entryway. The friends had tried to move as many as they could, throwing them to safety while keeping the monster at bay. But there had already been a number of casualties. A number that was sure to triple if the ceiling actually did collapse.

"I could try to burn it again," she offered, knees buckling as the floor beneath them rocked.

Dylan caught her, holding her close to his side. For a moment, he seemed to be considering. Then he gazed around the entryway and shook his head. "If you do and it takes off running, it's going to set the entire castle on fire. That's too big a risk."

"Then what do we do?" she asked anxiously.

The troll wasn't winding down; it was staying at a constant level of catastrophe. When it saw them looking, it let out a hair-raising scream and threw a chunk of marble. They ducked just in time.

"Any bright ideas?" Aidan appeared suddenly by their side. Vampires were gifted with extra-ordinary endurance, but even he was panting. The majority of the civilian relocation had been left to him and he'd been dodging the monster at the same time. "It's not just going to die on principle."

Dylan's eyes flickered up to its chest, then kept moving all the way to its mottled head.

"You feeling really, *really* thirsty?"

Aidan shot him a choice look.

"...it was worth a shot."

Time was running out. The longer the beast thrashed about, the greater the chance it was going to take one of the friends down with it. They had to do something. They had to—

A single arrow shot into the air.

The friends watched as it went higher and higher. Missing the troll entirely. Whispering almost out of sight. Until, all at once, it sliced through its target with a quiet *ping*.

There was a collective gasp. A severed chain swung back and forth. And a five-hundred-year-old chandelier fell down from the ceiling...

...right on top of the monster's head.

The shockwave that followed knocked Katerina right off her feet. She flew backwards along with the rest of them as the troll's body cratered into the ground. The sound alone was enough to make her eyes water, but just as suddenly all was quiet and still.

She and the others lifted their heads, staring through the clouds of dust, only to see the crown prince kneeling on the stairs—a silver bow still clutched in his hand.

Kailas.

Katerina blinked slowly, unable to believe her eyes. It was over. The beast was dead.

A breathless cheer rang out from the others as she sank down where she stood. Somewhere on the verge of laughter and tears. Clutching at her fractured wrist all the while.

It's dead. It's actually dead. We're going to be okay.

Relief swept over her like a wave. Slowly loosening her muscles. Unlocking the knot that had formed in her chest. Her face was smeared with soot. She finally forced herself to pull in a breath.

"You were amazing," Dylan murmured, burying his face in her hair. One entire half of his body had been shredded by the monster's claws, but he didn't seem to notice. On the other side of the troll, Cassiel was tenderly lifting Tanya into his arms. "Absolutely amazing."

Katerina couldn't even answer. She just held on to him. Beaming from head to toe. A second later, she twisted around to thank their unlikely savior. Then she froze.

It took her a second to realize Kailas wasn't smiling. While the others danced and cheered her twin was just standing there, stricken with fear. It wasn't until she followed his gaze that she realized what had him frozen. That she realized why his handsome face was so frightfully pale.

Two more trolls were running across the bridge...

Chapter 2

The smiles froze on their faces. Echoes of their cheers still lingered in the hall, echoing off the walls.

Katerina watched them coming in what felt like slow motion. Their mottled flesh gleamed in the moonlight. A look of brutish determination was in their beady little eyes. Flecks of foaming drool splattered off of their bared teeth, and as they ran across the drawbridge it collapsed in their wake.

And there goes our escape.

This time, Cassiel took a step back. Then another. A muscle twitched in his jaw and she could practically see the wheels turning behind those dark eyes.

Then he and Dylan looked at each other. He shook his head.

"RUN!"

No sooner had the ranger shouted than they were all streaking up the shattered stairs to the second story. Sprinting in corsets and borrowed cloaks up both sides of the winding staircase. No one dared to look behind them, but at this point there was no need. They could track the trolls' progress as easily as if they were seeing it themselves. Listening as each crashing step got closer and closer.

Serafina's long hair whipped out in front of her. Aidan's fangs were bared. None of the rest of them had any weapons, but Katerina could see from the tension in Dylan's back that he was dying to shift.

You and me both!

If only it was possible, but Dylan was correct with what he said before. For her to shift within the castle was a death sentence to everyone inside. And she'd never make it to the courtyard in time. The trolls were already there.

"Look out!"

It was impossible to see or hear who was screaming. It was impossible to see much of anything through the giant chunks of marble and plaster that were falling on their heads.

Kailas was struck in the arm, and he stumbled back into the wall. Tanya got a glancing blow across the forehead, but continued barreling up the stairs.

With the building coming down around them, there was little other choice.

Just make it to the roof. Katerina lifted her gown and sprinted alongside her friends, sure they were all thinking the same thing. *Just make it to the roof, then I can shift and fly us out of here!*

If only it was that simple. However, the cave trolls had no intention of letting them leave.

Far from the lumbering beasts she would have imagined, the trolls were fast—each one of their quick strides matching more than ten of a normal man's. The impact of every thundering step was unimaginable, leaving six-foot craters in the tiled floor, and by the time they'd leapt over the carcass of their fallen compatriot the very foundations of the castle had begun to crack.

Just a little farther. Just a little bit farther...

Apparently it wasn't meant to be.

When the first beast leapt onto the stairs, she was thrown off her feet. By the time the second one joined it, the staircase itself splintered in half—throwing the friends in opposite directions.

"KAT!"

She heard Dylan call her name just as he and Tanya slipped over the broken railing, tumbling out of sight. A second later the ground shook again, and Kailas and Serafina went careening off in the other direction. A hand shot out of nowhere, pulling Katerina down as a blunted club shattered the stone where her head used to be, but before she could see who had grabbed her the floor beneath her vanished and she let out a piercing scream.

It wasn't the first time she'd fallen to an almost certain death, but it was by far the most terrifying. Each second seemed to happen in slow motion. Playing out like a dark dream.

Her hair flew up in a fiery cloud as her mouth opened in a silent scream. Her arms reached out above her, but there was no one left in sight. The floor beneath her roiled and churned as one of the trolls opened its gaping mouth—

—and came up empty.

"CASS!"

Katerina's arms wrapped around the fae's neck as he dove right off the ledge after her. His feet came down on the beast's forehead as he caught the young queen tightly in his arms. But before it could open its mouth again, they were leaping to freedom—landing on the broken ledge of the second story as the trolls and everything else beneath them fell back into dust.

The two friends clutched each other in the silence that followed. Katerina let out a tiny sneeze. And *that* is when all that supernatural adrenaline ran out.

Far from the usual graceful dismount Cassiel dropped her unceremoniously to the floor, staggering back to lean against the wall. The man had been killed, mauled, resurrected, and fought back a cave troll all in the same day. That legendary endurance was done.

"Thank you," Katerina panted, both hands on her knees. There was a split running up one side of her dress and the opposite sleeve had been torn clean off. "For catching me. And for pulling me down. That club would have decapitated me for sure."

"I didn't," he muttered, nursing a bloody lip. "I couldn't see who that was, but it wasn't me."

She thought about that for a moment, then nodded.

"In that case... thanks for nothing."

He glanced at her swiftly, then his lips cracked into a weak smile.

"You've been spending too much time with us."

It was a lesson she'd learned early on. That forced levity. In the beginning, she'd found it borderline macabre. But it was a survival tactic just as surely as any amount of training.

"Just part of my natural charm." She tugged lightly on what was left of his shirt. "Come on, we've got to find the others. Dylan and Tanya fell down to the lower levels, Sera and Kailas are still on the ground floor with the trolls, and I didn't even see what happened to Aidan—"

"Hang on." He caught her swiftly and pulled her back, gazing down the hallway with her tucked protectively against his side. "We still don't know what's up here."

Sure enough, they stood there listening for only a moment before the silence was shattered by a loud *CRASH.* The same sound they were going to investigate in the first place. Whatever had been making it hadn't been deterred by the arrival of the trolls. It had barely even noticed.

The two of them shared a quick look before cautiously venturing forward together.

All of Cassiel's weapons had been spent on the troll, and Katerina seriously doubted she had enough strength to make so much as a campfire. Not that either one wanted to dwell on any of that.

Still, it was hard to completely tune out that impending sense of doom.

"Cass, remember your silver dagger?" Katerina whispered suddenly, fighting the urge to cling to his hand. "The one that went missing our first week back? I accidentally dropped it in the river when Dylan and I were out riding. Sorry."

There was a hitch in the fae's step as he cast her an incredulous look.

"What is this, deathbed confessions?!"

"I'm just saying—"

"Well *stop* saying it!" The man looked like he'd been repeatedly dropped from a particularly nasty cliff, but you'd never know it from that unswerving indignation. "We don't prepare for the worst, we don't make peace, or give up! I'll throttle you for that dagger just as soon as we get out of this, and don't think for a second that I'm going to for-get—"

That's when a door burst open.

That's when the crashing stopped.

And that's when everything started to go horribly wrong.

The thing that sprang out into the hallway was unlike anything Katerina had ever seen. Over twelve feet tall, but it was coiled. Dark. Leaning on what looked like they used to be wrists, but had now sharp-ened into a single, deadly point. The dark sinews running over its body contracted as it sucked in a breath. It had no eyes, but turned its face towards them with a series of insectoid clicks.

Nine coils of teeth spiraled out of its head. Each one longer than Katerina's arm.

It's a monster.

She could think of no other word. The thing was a monster. And not the kind that hid beneath your childhood bed or plagued your waking dreams. This was so, *so* much worse.

"Cass...?"

She reached for the fae, but he was frozen perfectly still—staring at the creature like it was his own nightmare come to life. It reared up on its hind legs, letting out an unearthly cry, but he didn't move a muscle. He just stared in breathless terror, arms hanging limply at his sides.

Then it started to run.

"CASS—LOOK OUT!"

Katerina looked on in horror as the monster blurred towards them, body coiling in on itself, galloping in disjointed bursts of speed. Cassiel just stood there. He didn't even lift his hands. The ground shook as it took to the air, claws reaching towards him, letting loose another ser-rated cry—

Then it vanished in a burst of flames.

The queen tackled the fae around the waist, shoving him to safety while shooting a spray of liquid fire out of her hands. The flames wrapped around the beast like they had a mind of their own, twisting and writhing, absorbing its screams.

A second later it fell to the ground. Twitching as its body crumbled to ash.

Katerina stared at it for a moment before turning to Cassiel. He was lying in a breathless pile in the middle of the hall, looking like he'd seen a ghost.

"What the heck is wrong with you?!"

His eyes flashed up to hers, stricken beyond words. "I...I don't..."

There's no time.

There was another crash at the end the corridor and, having seen it up close, she was suddenly certain the creature that attacked them was incapable of making such a sound.

Without stopping to think she darted forward and grabbed the fae, yanking him to his feet and pulling him down the hall. He followed with a sort of helpless obedience. Skittering around the smoldering remains the way a spider frightened a child. They darted into the first room that was available, and the second they were inside he collapsed against the door.

"I'm sorry," he panted, running his hands over his face. "I'm sorry."

Katerina just stood there, completely at a loss as to what to do. Just moment earlier, she'd seen the man fly around the castle entryway in a dazzling display of deadly acrobatics. He'd leapt into the abyss just to catch her, coming down on the open jaws of a cave troll.

And then...

CRASH!

Her breathing hitched as her eyes flickered automatically to the door. The same door the fae was still cringing against like the world was about to end. "What can I do to get you past this?"

"I'm past it," he said quickly. With visible effort he shook off whatever trauma was haunting him, pulling back his long hair and squaring his shoulders. "I'm past it."

Yeah. Right.

CRASH!

"What IS that!" Katerina asked in exasperation. She'd puzzle over the fae's strange antics later. Right now, there simply wasn't time. "I think it's coming from—"

But a second later, they both saw where it was coming from.

Because a second later it walked right inside.

The queen and fae froze in surprise as the closet door opened and a shrouded figure stepped out. For a second, Katerina could have sworn it was human. Only its blood-red hands tipped her off that something was wrong. It hadn't seen them yet, too focused on its task. A task which appeared to be overturning every piece of furniture in the five kingdoms.

What the—?!

Little shrieks and snarls of frustration ripped past its lips as it continued its frantic path of destruction. Opening drawers. Kicking open chests. It wasn't until it shattered a vase on the floor that Katerina realized it was searching for something.

And it wasn't until Cassiel lodged a shard of glass in its back that it finally stopped.

The hood of the shroud fell away as it whirled around with a shriek, staring at them with a pair of sightless blood-red eyes. Its veined mouth opened with a strange sucking sound, sampling the air, before it shrieked again—vibrating from head to toe.

Why is everything in this nightmare dimension blind?

"Get back, Katerina," Cassiel warned grimly, holding up a piece of the closet door like a shield. "It's a Kaelar."

"What's that?" she asked nervously, woefully behind when it came to fictitious monsters that suddenly decided to come to life. "What can it do?"

No sooner had she asked than the creature let out a screeching wail, showering the room in an acidic crimson spray. Everywhere the drops touched sizzled and burned. Eating their way through the carpet before finally sputtering out when they reached the floorboards below.

It was a kind of self-destruct. Whatever had rained down was the same substance that had dyed the creature red—leaving nothing but a melted-looking shroud in its wake. Fortunately, Cassiel seemed to have been expecting it. He deflected the bulk of it with the broken door.

"...that."

He threw what was left into the corner, careful not to get any on his hands. With a look of supreme disgust, he then stamped cautiously on the smoldering cloak. It was empty and still.

Katerina watched the whole thing with wide eyes, feeling like she'd stumbled into a dark reflection of her old world. A place fraught with terrifying dangers and even more terrifying beasts. A place where she didn't know the rules. Her only comfort was that she wasn't alone.

"You're past it?"

Her eyes locked with Cassiel, who was looking far more like the immortal warrior she was used to and far less like the frightened teenager who'd frozen in the hall.

He met her gaze for only a moment, then nodded. "I'm past it."

Okay, then.

Together, they made their way back into the hall. The rhythmic crashing had stopped—whatever a 'Kaelar' was, there appeared to be only one. But the second they stepped out of the room no less than three of the nightmare creatures from before sprang out to greet them.

"Cass?" Katerina asked nervously, backing up against the wall. "I don't think I can..."

He never broke eye contact as he stepped slowly in front of her, reaching out to pull a sword from the belt of a frozen soldier.

"Stay behind me."

The creatures charged with a piercing scream, only this time the fae was ready for them. The battle that followed was too fast for the queen to make sense of. A twirling, dizzying array of teeth and blades. It was more vicious than she could have imagined. A fantastical blur of death and speed.

And then it was over.

The creatures were lying in pieces on the floor. The fae was standing over them. Still breathing, but looking decidedly the worse for wear, his sword dripping dark, curdled blood.

"Are you okay?" Katerina rushed forward, trying to see where he'd been injured.

It wasn't easy to tell. Her boyfriend had taken great care to rip apart most every piece of him less than an hour before. It was a grim reality Cassiel seemed to be remembering at the same time.

He tentatively lifted the arm with the sword but it dropped, trembling, back to his side. "Dylan," he cursed between gritted teeth, swiftly swapping hands. "Why must he always—"

"He thought you were dying," Katerina snapped.

She was also going to mention how his fatigue might have something to do with the fact that he'd brought down a trio of demonic monstrosities, but one look at his face and she reconsidered.

"I *was* dying," he said irritably. "That doesn't mean he had to bite me so hard." A splatter of blood rained down from his shoulder as they ventured down the hall once more. "Honestly, it'll be a miracle if I don't turn into a mutt myself..."

It was with the greatest caution that they made their way slowly through what was left of the northern wing of the castle. They ran into several more nightmarish creatures along the way, but between the fae's inborn resilience and the fact that the queen was able to shoot fire out of her hands they were able to dispatch them and escape relatively un-scathed.

It wasn't until they reached her room at the top of the tower that they faced a dilemma.

"Go out the window," Cassiel instructed, sliding a bureau over to barricade the door the second they'd stepped inside. "Climb up to the roof, then shift and get out of here. Fly east to the sanctuary, or Belaria, or Vale. Tell them what happened. Tell them to send reinforcements."

Katerina froze where she stood, then folded her arms across her chest.

"And let me guess, you'll stay behind and battle the darkness alone? Slay the beasts, save our friends, and rescue the castle from its evil curse?"

The Fae prince continued his furniture stacking, completely oblivi-ous to the sarcasm in her tone. "Yes, precisely."

Unbelievable.

"Is that something they actually teach in Fae-school? That inflated sense of self?" she asked with a withering glare. "Or is it unique to you and what's left of your delusional family?"

He straightened up slowly, turning around with honest surprise. "Katerina, if you're worried about the climb I can help you—"

She threw a shoe at his face. That was the last talk of splitting up.

"I still don't see why you wanted us to come here," he said testily, sinking down onto the bed as she rifled through her drawers. "We should be doubling back to the—"

"Cass, what're you doing?!" she demanded, seeing him reclining there for the first time. "You're bleeding like crazy! Get off my bed!"

He glanced down at the sheets for a moment before looking up in disbelief. "Are you serious? Those trolls knocked the southern turret straight through the dining room wall, but you're worried I might be staining the sheets?"

She gestured to the room in exasperation.

"If you hadn't noticed, this is one of the only places that escaped damage." She stalked forward, snatching a throw pillow out of his hands. "Everything is exactly as it should be, so if you don't mind…"

The fae stared up at her for a moment then pushed stiffly to his feet, muttering what she assumed were dark profanities in his native tongue. She followed his progress with grim satisfaction, placing the pillow snugly back into place.

"…shouldn't be in my bed in the first place," she sniffed, stuffing a small chest deep into the pocket of her gown. "Aren't you the one always carrying on about our newfound royal propriety?"

"Why not?" A flash of dark humor shot through his eyes. "We are betrothed, are we not? You should get used to the sight of me in your bed."

She froze for a split second then moved to the window, shaking her head. "…that was the scariest moment of this entire day."

He laughed shortly, following her to the ledge. "Nothing like a little gallows humor…"

Together, they stuck their heads out the window and peered out at the drop below. The queen could have sworn they'd only just gotten to the castle an hour or so before, but the sun was already coming up over the tips of the trees—painting the sky with an ironically radiant glow.

"So what's the plan here, princess?"

Like Aidan, he'd taken her coronation as less of a title change than a quaint way to pass the time. She shot him a rueful grin, then gestured to a crevice by the southern wall.

"You see that little tunnel? Under the hollyhock?"

He squinted for a moment, then nodded. "The drainage ditch?"

"It's a tunnel," she repeated. "It leads into the dungeon."

He pulled back in surprise, eyebrows lifting to his hair, before gazing down at the flowering plants once more. "Well, *that's* a useful bit of information…"

She rolled her eyes, resisting the urge to give him a hard shove. "You're not fighting against the House of Damaris anymore, remember? You can stop jotting things down for your evil plan."

"Never hurts to be prepared."

She purposely ignored this. The same way she ignored it when he and his kinsmen were taking mental notes on the precise height and shape of the battlements when they first arrived.

"Anyway, the plan is to get down there and see if we can find Dylan and Tanya."

The names sobered him and he studied the tunnel with a slight frown. "You think they're down there?"

She bit her lip, refusing to think otherwise. "That's the direction they went flying, so that's where we have to look. They could be hurt, or trapped. There's no other alternative."

His eyes softened as he gazed down at her. A second later he gently squeezed her hand. "We're going to find them, Kat. They're going to be all right." When she finally lifted her chin, his lips pulled up in a crooked smile. "They always are."

That's true.

No matter the circumstances, she and her friends had the uncanny knack to survive.

"Okay." She squared her shoulders, pulling in a deep breath. "So we go down together."

He nodded and glanced over the side. After a few seconds, when she said nothing further, he shot her a discreet look. "Did you have a plan for doing that, or..."

Their eyes met and she looked up at him hopefully. There was a heavy pause.

"Your plan was to ask me."

Her face broke into a radiant smile, thrilled he'd caught on so fast. "Cass, it's like you can read my mind."

He laughed in quiet exasperation, rolling his eyes. "I take back everything I said in your bedroom. You and Dylan are perfect for each other."

"This is why we're such a great team."

Without a second of hesitation she leapt into his arms. Trusting that they'd always manage to hold her. Trust that her infallible friend would achieve the impossible and manage to save the day.

Her friends had an uncanny knack for that as well.

"Hold on tight," he cautioned, stepping out onto the ledge. One hand gripped her waist as the other ran along the high stone wall. "And if I were you, I'd close my eyes..."

Chapter 3

For the second time in less than a day, Katerina found herself dangling over open air. She fought back a scream, burying her face in the fae's neck while clutching at his rapidly fraying shirt. A shirt which promptly tore into shreds. She was sure he'd give her crap for it later, but at the moment she couldn't care less. She was far more concerned with things like gravity and the fact that, while she'd ascended the throne of the High Kingdom, she'd somehow neglected to make a will.

The wind was screaming in her ears. Her body flung weightlessly from side to side. Then the two of them dropped in sheer free fall, and for a fleeting moment she thought it was the end. Again.

"Kat?"

The fae looked down at the lovely girl who'd somehow managed to wrap her entire body around his chest. Her eyes were screwed up tight and her hair looked as though she'd been struck by lightning then dropped from a cliff. He shook his head patiently. *Mortals could be such children.*

"Kat...?" He gently loosened her chokehold, peeling back her arms and allowing himself a moment to breathe. "You can let go now, we're here."

Considering I fly around as a dragon, you'd think I'd have gotten over my fear of heights.

She clung to him like a monkey for another moment before toppling to the ground. The second she landed her knees buckled and she plopped onto the grass, blinking around in a daze. A throat cleared softly and she lifted her head to see him gazing down with a truly affectionate smile.

"Sweet girl, I was never going to let you..." His eyes darkened with rage as he looked down at himself for the first time. "What the—? What have you done to my clothes?!"

There it is.

With a little sigh she pushed awkwardly to her feet, taking great care to avoid his burning gaze. "I don't care what the council says, it would never have worked between us."

He shoved her back onto the grass, muttering under his breath as he tried to salvage what was left of his tunic. "You are the most intolerable girl I have ever met. Again—*perfect* for Dylan."

She snorted in laughter, and he glanced down in rage to see her staring up with a smile. A second later he was smiling himself, hating himself for it all the while.

"Oh, get up." In a gracious, if rather abrupt, movement he pulled her to her feet, wiping his hands afterwards with a scowl. "Clumsy little monster."

She righted herself with a grin, ruffling his hair for good measure.

Yep. Forced bits of levity. Only way to survive.

A sudden *clang* from inside the castle wiped their smiles clean away.

"Come on!" She grabbed his hand, pulling him beneath the canopy. "We have to hurry!"

They groped their way through the tangled underbrush for only a moment before coming up against the castle wall. Once they were there, Katerina's hands slid down with expert precision and found the latch to open the tiny rounded door. It was a tight squeeze but they both managed to make it inside, spilling out into the dark chamber underneath.

"Now what?" Cassiel muttered, keeping one step ahead of her in the dark.

She held on to the edge of his cloak, praying they wouldn't get lost. "Now is typically where Kailas and I would get scared and run away."

There was a pause.

"When was the last time you were down here?"

Another pause.

"I was about six years old."

The fae shook his head and continued down the shadowy corridor. "I have a great idea: you see that girl behind me, the one with all the brilliant plans? Let's crown her queen."

"I gave you back your kingdom, didn't I?" she replied scathingly.

"Oh *thank* you, Your Majesty. For returning a fifth of what should have been mine."

"Well, I'm sorry we didn't go with your genius plan," she shot back. "I fly off as a dragon and leave you here all by yourself. With my luck, you'd probably freeze up again—"

A hand clamped over her mouth.

"*Shh*—listen."

For a second, they stood there. Stock-still in the darkness. Waiting with bated breath. Then she heard it. The sound of two muffled voices coming from the end of corridor. Two voices that warmed them with unspeakable relief. Two voices that were bickering just as fiercely as they were.

The queen and the fae shared a quick look before hurrying down the hall.

"Outrageously immature."

"As if *now* is the time."

After a few unending moments, the corridor widened and Katerina found herself standing in the middle of the dungeon. A place she hadn't been since Cassiel's childhood friend had died in her arms writhing in agony, struck suddenly blind.

He seemed to remember it at the same time. For a second he paused, staring at the exact place where an eternal Fae had taken his last breath, then his eyes flickered quickly to the next cell.

"Tanya!"

Katerina followed his gaze, eyes resting not upon the tiny shape-shifter but on the beautiful man crouched in the darkness by her side.

Dylan.

She and Cassiel rushed forward, thrilled but a little confused by what they saw. Their friends didn't exactly look happy to see them. In fact, as backwards as it was, they looked remarkably upset.

"I'm glad to see you guys are taking it easy," Cassiel remarked, eyeing their reclined position in the back of the cell. "You get that you're on the wrong side of the cage, right?"

There was no time for a pithy comeback. The second he'd spoken Dylan leapt to his feet, staring in terror over the back of his friend's head.

"LOOK OUT!"

A deafening growl rocketed off the walls as the door swung open and the two friends darted inside. It flew shut just a massive body slammed against it. Screaming to all hell. Gnashing its teeth.

Katerina straightened up slowly, staring in disbelief.

"Is that...?"

"It's a Carpathian lion," Dylan panted, holding the door shut with all his might. Cassiel was quick to help him. Fortunately, while the beast might have been gigantic, it had yet to discover the wonders of opposable thumbs. "And, yeah, it's actually that big."

Katerina shook her head slowly, fighting off the waves of shock. "No...no, you told me there were no animals in Carpathia. You specifically said—"

"That's because, just like everything else about that wretched land, the animals weren't normal," Dylan replied breathlessly. "They grew so feral, even the Carpathians couldn't handle them. They had to wipe them all out."

The lion roared again and the four friends cowered in the back of the cell.

Yeah—I'd wipe them out, too.

"So how are we going to fight it?" she asked in a whimper.

Dylan shook his head, looking decidedly pale. "We're not going to fight it. We're going to stay here forever. It's already been decided."

"Why don't you shift?" Cassiel demanded.

"That's what *I* said," Tanya muttered.

"As a *wolf*?!" Dylan shot back. "You want me to fight that thing as a *wolf*?!"

"...and that's what *he* said."

"We can't fight it otherwise," Cassiel replied, in what he clearly deemed his most rational voice. "We don't have any weapons."

Dylan's eyes flashed with anger. "Then why don't you use your bare hands, Cass? That's what you're telling *me* to do!"

"Guys, this isn't helping—"

The lion roared again and they all fell silent. After a few seconds, Cassiel took a step back.

"I agree with Dylan. We stay in the cell."

The ranger smirked, while Katerina threw up her hands. "Oh, come on! There has to be something we can do!"

"I'm all ears, princess."

Dylan never adhered to royal titles. She had been 'princess' to him since the moment they met. She shot him an exasperated glare, while Tanya traced the ground with her toe.

"I suggested we sacrifice your boyfriend..."

The room erupted into arguing once more, echoing loudly off the walls, before a pair of new voices joined the rest. Calling in confusion. Getting closer by the second.

"Cass, is that you?"

The fae froze, staring down the hallway in dread.

"Katy!" Only one person in the world used that name. "Katy, are you down here?"

It was quiet for a split second, they everyone started shouting at once.

"Guys, get out of here!"
"There's a lion! Go back!"
"Sera—RUN!"
"Get back upstairs!"

Unfortunately, the newest additions to their gang were just as stubborn as the rest. Just a few seconds later, Serafina's pale face ducked into view. Kailas was soon to follow.

When both of them had fallen off the staircase, they landed back on the ground floor. Just the two of them...along with those pesky trolls. How they had managed to survive was a straight-up miracle, but staring at them in the darkness it was clear that survival had come at a price.

There wasn't an inch of Kailas that wasn't bleeding. Several long spikes were embedded in his shoulders and most all the skin had been scraped off the back of his hands. Serafina hadn't fared much better. While the lovely fae had pioneered the term 'warrior princess', she had clearly met her match. Her dress was torn. Her face was ripped and bleeding. And the arm that wasn't holding the shaking torchlight was clutched tight against her chest.

The couple stared into the dungeon for only a moment. Then they saw the lion.

"Oh freakin' eh!!" Kailas yelled, springing back up the stairs.

Serafina tried to follow, but the beast sprang immediately into her path. The torch fell from her hands, clattering to the ground before vanishing into smoke as her brother threw himself against the bars of the cell—pulling on the door with all his might.

"Sera!" he called, trying to pry open the bent iron. "Hang on—I'm coming!"

It was impossible to see through the darkness, and it was impossible to open the door to the cell. The weight of the lion had warped the metal, driving it deep into the stone. In a blind panic, the four friends threw themselves repeatedly against the bars—listening in cold terror to a discordant symphony of screams mixed with the lion's bloodthirsty roar.

It was too terrible to imagine. Worse than if they'd been seeing it with their own eyes.

Dylan's shoulder broke as he slammed it against the bars of the cell. Cassiel was yelling so desperately, he didn't realize he'd ripped open all the skin on his hands; they slipped and tore against the rusted iron. A second later, Katerina could swear she saw bone.

Then, all at once, the room went quiet.

The four friends backed slowly into the cell. Staring blindly into the dark. Hands cupped over mouths as they waited, hardly daring to breathe.

If it was possible, the silence was worse than the screams. Katerina could only imagine what it meant. Could only imagine the broken bodies strewn across the floor in the dark.

Then suddenly—

"Run!"

Cassiel saw her first. His eyes were attuned to such things. One second he was frozen beside the rest of them, stricken with grief. The next, he was banging on the walls of the cage, urging his sister onward, waving desperately with his hand.

"Sera, run!"

The others joined him, watching with bated breath as the fae streaked down the center of the dungeon—the lion right at her heels.

Seven hells...I can't watch.

Katerina covered her mouth as the giant cat leapt into the air, reaching towards the princess with outstretched claws. But Serafina hadn't survived for years in the Damaris dungeon just to die within its walls. A second before the beast could touch her, she spiraled gracefully across the ground—sliding just inches beneath its savage fangs before crashing to safety in one of the cells.

...the same cell she'd been trapped in before.

She picked herself up slowly, checking to make sure she had all her limbs, before glancing around the bars of the cage. "...well, this is ironic."

Her brother let out a choking gasp of laughter but Katerina pushed past him, hands curled around the twisted iron, searching for a brother of her own.

"Kailas!" she shouted, waiting desperately for a response. "Kailas, can you hear me?"

Dylan walked up slowly behind her, putting a tentative hand on her shoulder. She shook it off—refusing to be comforted, refusing to admit he might be dead. A part of her had wished him dead for the last ten years. She was just getting used to the idea of wanting him alive.

"KAILAS!" she screamed again, eyes scanning the darkness.

Serafina had frozen perfectly still, realizing he wasn't with her for the first time.

"He went...he went up the stairs," she said quietly, not noticing her entire body had started to tremble. "He went back up the stairs; he's not..."

But Kailas would never have left her behind.

And they'd all heard his screams mixed in with the rest.

"Kat..." Tanya took her friend by the hand, shaking her head in disbelief as a stream of silent tears poured down her face. "I'm sorry. I can't even...I'm so, *so* sorry."

But Katerina wasn't having it. She wrenched herself away, screaming into the dark.

"KAILAS ALEXANDER DAMARIS—YOU SHOW YOURSELF THIS INSTANT!"

You can't do this to me. Not again. I cannot lose you again.

"KAILAS!"

For a minute, nothing happened. For a full minute, the queen's heart stood still.

Then a tall man came sprinting out of the shadows.

YES!

Robbed of its prize, the lion was prowling on the other side of the dungeon. If he hurried, there was a chance the prince could actually make it to safety.

But Kailas had no intention of joining his friends.

He had every intention of getting them out.

"Here," he instructed as he pried an ancient sconce off the wall, passing it through the bars of the cage to Dylan, "try to wedge it open with this."

He cast a quick look over his shoulder, oblivious to their shell-shocked faces.

"Hurry."

For a second, nobody moved. Then Katerina gave her boyfriend a little shove.

"You heard the man," she echoed with a breathless grin. "Wedge it open."

The ranger did as he was asked, and a few seconds later each one of the friends was levelling themselves against the iron—pushing with all their might.

"That's it," Kailas breathed, shoulder braced against the wall. Serafina had already escaped her own cage and was standing behind him. "Just a little bit more—"

"Kailas!" she cried.

The prince looked over his shoulder, staring into the darkness as the Carpathian lion bounded down the hall. Its eyes locked not on himself, but on the beautiful woman by his side.

Katerina would remember those next few seconds as long as she lived. Each fractured snapshot was forever immortalized in her mind.

The way her brother pushed Serafina instinctively to safety, not hesitating for a moment to take her place. The way his hands flew up as the lion leapt towards him.

That final look on his face.

The look of sheer astonishment as a wave of fire flew from his hands.

NO ONE HAD EVER KILLED a Carpathian lion. It was said even the queen couldn't do it. The only way they exterminated the beasts was by having a dark sorcerer lead them over the side of a cliff.

No one had ever actually killed one... until today.

At least, that's was Cass told them. And Kat believed him.

It was quiet. Scary quiet. Like most things the prince did that were sudden or unexpected, this one was met with a great deal of caution—even fear. Because he wasn't supposed to have his powers. Alwyn was supposed to have taken his powers away.

But Alwyn died. So what happens then?

They came back, apparently. Returned to their rightful owner.

And just in the nick of time.

It was a silence no one seemed to know how to break, and as much as she wanted to give her twin the benefit of the doubt, Katerina found herself as paralyzed as the rest of them.

Seconds ticked by, each as unbearable as the next.

Then, in an act of comradery the queen had yet to understand, Dylan clapped her brother on the shoulder and stepped out of the cell. "...okay then."

Okay then?

One by one, the others followed—each tagging on their own understated words of support.

"Nice work."

"Keep it up."

"You've got some lion on your jacket."

Serafina gave him a soft kiss on the cheek before heading out after Tanya—giving the lion's head a vengeful kick as she walked past. Soon, only her brother was left.

Unlike the others, Cassiel had gone very still.

As relieved as he was to be free Kailas Damaris had garnered his fearsome reputation for a reason, and at the expense of many lives. Cassiel was watching him now the same way he'd looked at the entrance to the tunnel. The same way he'd counted the battlements on the wall.

"Cass—come on!"

The handsome fae blinked out of his trance, giving the prince a curt nod as he slipped past into the dungeon. Casting a silent glance back over his shoulder. A glance no one else saw.

And then there were two.

The twins looked at each other awkwardly before Kailas cocked his head self-consciously down the hall. The two of them walked down together. Not speaking, but standing very close.

It wasn't until they reached the end that Katerina shot him a sideways glance. "I didn't know you could do that," she said softly.

A faint shiver raced up the prince's arms. He bowed his head. "Neither did I."

The two shared a fleeting look. One that spoke volumes. One that was cut short by Tanya's frantic cry, "Where's Aidan?"

The friends circled around each other, as accusatory as they were distressed.

"I thought he was with you."

"We saw him go with *you*!"

Serafina shook her head. "Kailas and I haven't seen him since he pulled Katerina out of the way on the stairs."

So that was him. I should have known it was him.

"Well, he's got to be somewhere." Dylan's eyes flickered up to the ceiling. "We'll look for him together—no one goes off on their own. The second we find him, we get the hell out of..."

He trailed off, those shifter senses stilling with sudden attention. A second later Katerina heard it, too. The sound of a violent battle. The sound of a man fighting for his life.

Seven hells...here we go again.

Chapter 4

It was happening in a ballroom.

Maybe it was for the irony. Maybe it was simply for the this-can't-get-anymore-unbelievable scale.

The six friends raced up the dungeon stairs, searching for their seventh. Although each of them was clearly on their last leg, they fought back whatever evils sprang out to greet them. Hooded changelings. Skeletal manticores. Reanimated cadavers—twisted and warped beyond recognition.

By the time they reached the ground floor, Katerina had tears in her eyes. Not just from the pain, but from the echoes and images of everything she'd seen. Things that she'd never be able to forget. Things that were sure to haunt her for years to come.

If we make it out of this alive.

"Come on." Dylan grabbed her with one hand, fending off some kind of rabid boar with the other. "We're almost there."

The queen floated beside him in a kind of daze, watching as two ghouls threw themselves at Tanya, then promptly forgot what they were doing and started eating each other alive.

"...I'm going to be sick."

Her stomach lurched and he glanced back at her, his blue eyes shining with panic.

"We're almost there," he said again, throwing a dagger at a shadowy figure flying towards them, only to have it dissolve into smoke. "Just hang on a second..."

The six of them screeched to a stop.

"...longer."

It was like some sort fairytale, turned dark and upside-down. The ballroom was full of people, just like Katerina had seen it a million times before. Granted, these ones were hardly dancing and you couldn't really call them people.

At a glance, they looked human enough. Same proportions, same approximate shape. But when you looked closer, there was nothing human about them.

Their skin wasn't skin at all, but bands of dark, sinewy muscle—much like the creatures that had attacked her and Cassiel upstairs. Their limbs were thin and stretched, reaching much farther than they were supposed to and their fingers ended in razor-sharp claws. Their heads were bald, though each one was wearing the same dark cloak, and the air itself seemed to hiss every time they moved.

"Kasi demons," Dylan breathed, freezing in the entryway. "I've never seen so many..."

There had to be more than three hundred of them. That's how many people the ballroom was supposed to hold, and the place was packed to the brim. They stood in a giant circle, fifty or so deep. Swaying slightly with that unearthly hiss, all turned to face the same direction.

And there was Aidan, standing in the middle of it all.

The queen had never seen such devastating odds. And never had she seen so much blood.

Most of it belonged to the Kasis, but the vampire had contributed plenty as well. His only salvation was that no more than fifteen could charge him at a time. There simply wasn't room.

That's what was keeping him alive. That he was fighting no more than *fifteen* at a time.

In the name of all that was good and holy, she had no idea how he was still breathing.

How is he doing this?!

Again and again the demons flew forward. Again and again he drove them back. Paying a higher price each time. They weren't designed to need weapons, but they used them anyway. Striking and stabbing and slashing, while Aidan used his bare hands. His speed was impossible, but no matter how many he killed ten more flooded forward to take their place. They were fighting to kill. He was fighting only to escape. But escape wasn't an option, and it was only a matter of time.

Even vampires weren't invincible, and Aidan was tiring fast. Bleeding even faster.

As the friends slid to a stop in the entryway, gawking in horror, one of the creatures slashed a knife across his face. A brutal attack, but one he could have easily dodged any other day.

He pulled back with a cry, and a chorus of chilling laughter rose up from the horde.

It had become sport to them. They didn't care about their own casualties, about the grisly body-count stacking up at the vampire's feet. They were interested only in the inevitable ending.

The one that was drawing closer and closer with every breath.

There was another soft cry and Aidan dropped to one knee. Clutching painfully at his shoulder. Wrenching out the spearhead that was buried inside.

Katerina let out a quiet gasp.

It wasn't the blood that frightened her. It was what happened after.

He isn't able to heal.

"HEY!"

She didn't think, she just screamed. Anything to get them to stop. Anything to get their attention. A childish attempt, but it ended up working a little too well.

A second later, all three hundred Kasi turned their way.

"In case I forget to tell you later," Tanya muttered, "you're an idiot."

Silly shifter. There's not going to BE a later.

Then they charged.

IT WAS PANDEMONIUM. No other way to describe it.

Bodies were flying everywhere. Limbs were tangling together. Katerina's very first thought was that she was glad they were all wearing the same dark cloak—it gave her something to swing at.

Her next thought was less of a coherent word and more of an internal scream.

Aidan!

The spear had been the final straw and he wasn't getting up. One hand was still desperately trying to stem the bleeding from his shoulder as the other raised protectively in front of his face.

A swarm of Kasi had flooded towards the friends when they arrived, but there was still a thick crowd gathered around the fallen vampire. Kicking at every inch of his broken body. Hissing in delight. Watching him slowly bleed out on the floor.

Stay down, Aidan. I'll just aim high.

She wasn't sure if it was their shared blood connection, or if the vampire simply knew her well enough to guess what she was going to do. But the second he saw her charging through the crowd, he abandoned all attempts to defend himself and dropped to the floor.

He'd only just covered his head when a wall of fire swept over him.

The swarm of Kasi let out a unified scream. Flailing around in agony, trying desperately to shed their flaming cloaks. She couldn't tell how many of them she had incapacitated or killed, but she *could* tell that Dylan had been right. Those flames might have just saved Aidan's life, but she couldn't risk using them like that a second time. Already some demons had begun to break off, falling against the walls and doorways. If she wasn't careful, the whole castle would catch fire.

But that didn't mean she had to stop using it altogether. It was just as effective short range.

"Laugh at *this*," she muttered as a massive demon stepped into her path. She felled it with a single hand, burning a hole right where its face used to be. Another leapt at her from behind but her fingers wrapped around its throat, flaming red-hot, tightening their hold until there was nothing left.

It was only then that she was able to see what a Kasi looked like up close. Scarier than the elongated limbs, or charcoaled skin, or the fact that they didn't have mouths so much as a row of outward-facing teeth—the demon's eyes were black as night. No color whatsoever.

And this point, I should be grateful they have eyes at all.

"Aidan!"

She leapt over the sea of mangled bodies and fell to her knees by his side, the hem of her dress instantly soaking through with a mixture of demon and vampire blood. There were still plenty of Kasi circling around them, but at the moment they were distracted by a giant Belarian wolf.

"It's okay," she gasped, pulling his head into her lap. "You're going to be okay!"

There was no longer a trace of color in his face; he was the exact shade of the ivory walls. Waves of dark hair were tangled over his forehead, and the random splashes of crimson were almost startling in contrast—like blood spilled onto fresh snow.

It was utterly heartbreaking. Yet somehow, he had never looked more beautiful.

Vampires were designed like that, he'd told her once. A biological safeguard to attract their prey when they were no longer able to hunt themselves. To draw them in closest at the very end.

"What can I do?" she whispered, stroking back his hair. "Tell me what to do."

The rest of him might have been broken, but his eyes were exactly the same. Sparkling up at her as if lit by some inner star. Almost painfully beautiful. Almost painfully bright.

"...Kat?"

Unsure whether he was awake or dreaming, he reached weakly for her hand. Their fingers laced together. Hers were burning hot, his were frightfully cold.

"Here." She started to roll up her sleeve, when the whole thing tore off in her hand. Without batting an eye, she dropped it onto the floor—offering out her wrist. "Drink."

The wolf glanced over his shoulder, then threw himself at the demons anew.

"I can't." Aidan pushed her arm away with the strength of a sickly child, hand falling back to the floor as soon as it finished the task. "I won't...I won't be able to stop."

Each breath was more ragged than the last. A bit of that light had begun to fade from his eyes. Yet he was worried about her safety.

"*Drink*," she said again, forcing her wrist to his mouth. "You'll die otherwise."

It seemed like just yesterday the roles were reversed. He was saying the same thing to her as she bled out from a panther attack in the middle of a swamp.

Still, he refused. On some things, the vampire would never compromise. The safety of the people he'd decided to love was top of that list.

"I'll kill you."

His eyes burned into hers, and she somehow knew it was true. But he was forgetting that she had a little supernatural assist of her own. Watching him deliberately the entire time, she placed a hand on his chest—her fingers glowing with heat.

"I'll stop you."

His face froze, considering it for the first time. Another wave of pain tore through him, and without seeming to think he reached tentatively for her arm, pulling it closer.

"Do it before you think you have to," he warned.

"Just drink."

At that point, survival instinct took over. He didn't need to be told again.

A sharp sting laced up the inside of her wrist. One that brought as much pleasure as it did pain. A strong tug was soon to follow, the pull of her blood as he drank deeply from the vein. Her arm began to tingle and shake, but at that point she was too distracted to notice.

It was sensation. Pure sensation.

Her eyes closed as her head bowed down to her chest. A Kasi demon flew up behind her, a battle-axe raised behind its head, but it was shot down without her ever knowing. She was in a different place now. Lost in the endless depth of that connection.

And she wasn't the only one.

Without her noticing Aidan slipped his hand behind her neck, his fingers wrapping through her hair, lips caressing the torn edges of her skin. A moment later, he lowered her gently to the floor. While she got weaker, he got stronger. Rising up above her. Pressing his body onto hers.

Until a red-hot burn shot through his chest.

He jerked away with a start. Fangs still bared, dripping her blood onto the floor. There was a wild light in his eyes, one she'd never seen before. For a moment, she thought he might actually bite her again. But with what looked like supreme effort, he made himself back away.

"I'm sorry," he said quietly, wiping his mouth. The fangs retracted. A flash of pain tightened his face, and they both watched as his shoulder stitched itself back together. He was almost bouncing now. Vibrating with an internal flush.

"...it's okay," she whispered.

She knew Aidan was a vampire. She knew, in theory, what vampires could do.

But *this*?

The two stared at each other across the floor. One was barely breathing. The other was unable to catch his breath. The battle raged on around them but they hardly even noticed, lost in their own world. As their eyes locked, time slowed. He made a compulsive movement towards her.

Then, all at once, he was pulled roughly to his feet.

"You okay?" Dylan asked shortly. His expression was perfectly neutral, but his eyes glowed with silent rage. As he waited for an answer, the hand on the vampire's shoulder clenched into a dangerous fist.

Aidan stared at him for a moment, then immediately dropped his eyes. "I'm fine. Thank you...Katerina."

Katerina? We're being formal now?

The queen pushed to her feet, feeling a little light-headed. "Anytime. I mean..." Both men looked at her, and she trailed off with a blush. "You know what I mean."

The fight was almost over. The horde had fallen back.

Tanya had shifted to look like a Kasi and was systematically decimating their ranks. Kailas had pulled the spikes from his shoulder and was stabbing them grimly through a demon's skull. As for the others, they were already making their way back to the main hall.

The long night was finally over. The dawn was finally within their reach.

"Let's go." Dylan grabbed her hand, pulling with a bit more force than necessary as he whisked her out of the ballroom. They had already reached the door before he called back to the stricken vampire, "You coming?"

Aidan blanched, then nodded quickly—blurring gracefully across the blood-soaked tile.

The castle had been cleared of those nightmares that haunted it. The others were already waiting, visibly aching to leave it all behind. There was just one thing they had to take care of first.

"Where are the trolls?" Cassiel asked.

It was the question everyone had been avoiding. The final card to be played.

"We locked them in the kitchen," Kailas answered quickly. His eyes lit up with the faintest bit of pride. "Don't worry, they can't get—"

There was an explosion of stone as the trolls burst into the room. "—out."

The gang shot him a withering look. The prince bowed his head. *Well, that didn't last long...*

A spiderweb of cracks shot over the remaining tiles as the beasts flew towards them. The drawbridge was already broken, and there was only one way in or out.

"What are we going to do?" Tanya asked anxiously, clutching the hilt of a spear. They all knew it wouldn't be enough. Nothing they had left was nearly enough.

Dylan stared for a moment, then squeezed Katerina's hand.

"Run for the door," he murmured. "Get outside and shift. Get out of here."

Her jaw clenched as her feet planted firmly on the floor. "I'm not leaving you."

The trolls were almost upon them. There were just seconds left. With some desperate instinct, the lot of them braced against the crumbling wall. Taking each other's hands.

If this was truly the end, then they would face it together.

Katerina's eyes closed. Her breath caught in her chest. A feeling of surreal detachment swept over her, and she found herself thinking the strangest thing.

I wish Dylan and I had gotten married.

Then a flash of light came down from the sky.

Katerina opened her eyes just in time to see the trolls fly towards each other—a look of pure shock eternally imprinted on their faces. They crashed together with the force of a dying star, letting out a joint wail before falling back to the earth—never to move again.

A sudden hush fell over the castle. The friends were frozen dead still. Then a gust of wind blew in from the shattered doorway and they all turned to see a tall woman standing in the frame.

"Oh dear," the woman said as she gazed out upon the tragic scene. "It seems I've come too late."

Petra?

Chapter 5

They made their way outside. None of them could stand to be in the castle another second.

As soon as they crossed over the threshold the door, broken as it was, sealed shut with a kind of hush. Katerina glanced back at it silently, remembering how it had done the same thing when she and Aidan headed into the forest the night before. They'd stepped outside at the precise moment the sun had touched down over the trees, silencing the castle with a whispered hush.

If they hadn't, maybe they'd be frozen with the rest of them.

"Petra!"

Katerina lifted her head as Aidan flew forward, catching the woman in an unexpected embrace. Unlike the rest of them he was completely uninjured, and apparently the heavy dose of her blood had left him slightly more exuberant than usual. Petra was the leader of the rebel camps. She was super strong, super powerful, and also Michael's sister.

Petra caught him in surprise, then lowered her hands affectionately to his back. "Dear boy."

As far as the queen knew, the two hadn't seen each other since battling Alwyn's dark forces that fateful night at the castle. But since leaving the rebel camp in Pora, where he'd been her first lieutenant, the vampire had spoken of her often—always with great admiration and respect.

He looked utterly relieved to see her now. More than that, Katerina actually *felt* the relief. It was rolling off him like a tide. Her face stilled to sudden attention and their eyes met.

A second later, he turned away.

"It looks as though you've all had quite a night."

Every witty reply fell short. Every clever answer died on their tongues. The friends were utterly spent, standing in a bedraggled line, suddenly looking very much their age.

Petra took in every detail, softening with an almost maternal concern. "You must rest," she commanded gently, snapping her fingers. A startlingly white stallion galloped out of the trees, saddle bags laden with the remainder of the supplies she'd brought for her journey. "Take what you need and sleep well. I suspect this is a long story, but there's no need for you to tell it now. I shall go into the castle and see for myself."

Into the castle?!

"No, you can't!" Katerina exclaimed. Her eyes darted frantically between the castle and the trees. "It isn't safe! We've been trying this whole time just to escape! There are creatures that…"

She trailed off, wondering why no one was protesting with her. Instead, they were all staring with the same amused smile. The general herself looked particularly amused.

"Petra will be fine," Dylan assured her quietly. "Trust me."

He spoke of her the same way he spoke of Michael. With that unconditional, infallible trust.

"I'll go with you," Aidan volunteered quickly, taking care to avoid the queen's eyes. "Show you the things we found. The people who are still frozen inside."

He's going back inside? He's really that desperate to get away from me?

She wouldn't have immediately guessed it but, again, she could literally *feel* his unease. It sharpened every time he looked at her. Every time he heard Dylan's voice.

"It's settled then." Petra pulled a long sword from the sheath on her belt, flipping it gracefully in her hand. "*Rest.* I'll be with you shortly. We can decide what to do from there."

Without a backwards glance, she headed towards the broken drawbridge—standing a foot taller the tall vampire walking by her side.

With every step, the shattered stone seemed to repair itself beneath her. Smoothing back together to look exactly as it had done before.

Katerina stared with wide eyes, unable to tear herself away.

"Did you see that?!" she demanded the second they disappeared inside. "Dylan, did you—"

But the handsome ranger was already asleep, stretched out in the grass beside the rest of her friends—all of whom were passed out cold. Katerina stared a moment, then lay down stiffly beside him. She understood the need for rest, but she didn't know how any of them could close their eyes.

Not with the things they'd seen. Not with the echoes still ringing in their ears.

A shudder ran up the queen's arms and she nestled closer to her boyfriend, lifting his arm and wrapping it snugly around her waist. You wouldn't catch her sleeping. Not in a hundred...

Her eyes fluttered shut and the world was quiet once more.

PETRA STILL WASN'T back by the time Katerina opened her eyes several hours later. Her first instinct was to be worried, but something about Dylan's tone set her mind at ease. She and her friends had already been through more than their share, bonding fast and close.

She'd learned to fear what they feared. To trust what they trusted.

He was still sleeping soundly by her side. One hand wrapped protectively around his left shoulder. The other twitching sporadically in his sleep. If she knew her man, he was back in that ballroom. Tearing apart every Kasi he might have missed. Bringing them back just so he could kill them all over again. Taking a swing at everyone who had done them harm.

...does that include Aidan?

The thought chilled her smile and she pushed silently to her feet. There was one person missing from their group. Coincidentally, it was the person she wanted to talk to the most.

Cassiel was sitting by himself on the bank of the river, not far from where he'd lost his life just a day before. He was still missing a shirt but his long cloak was tied around his shoulders, blowing gently in the breeze. Like always, he looked like a portrait. A very sad, fairytale portrait.

He didn't look up as she approached, but patted the grass at his side.

"How are you feeling?" she asked quietly, settling down beside him.

He ignored the question, keeping his dark eyes fixed on the castle walls. "I'm sorry... for freezing up back there." His musical voice tore at the edges of her heart. "I haven't felt something like that in a long time. I was unprepared."

It wasn't like him to apologize. Nor was it like him to show any weakness. But whatever happened back at the castle had laid him bare. Touched a raw nerve and reawakened old sorrow.

"...you'd seen one before?" she guessed hesitantly.

He bowed his head with a quiet sigh, shimmering strands of hair drifting gently across his face. "I had five sisters, did you know that?"

She stared at him, going very still. As a rule, the Fae didn't often speak of family. Probably because most of them had so little family left.

"Tanya mentioned something," she admitted. "Back at the sanctuary."

Cassiel has five sisters, she'd said. Then she corrected herself. *Had five sisters.*

"Aurelia was the oldest," he said softly. "Sera and I got into our fair share of trouble, but Aurelia made us look tame. She never did anything she didn't want to. I hero-worshiped her every step."

An ancient smile warmed the corners of his face.

"At only twenty years old, she was made captain of the guard. Her skills were unparalleled. I didn't know a single person who could have bested Aurelia in a fight."

There was a sudden pause.

"But Ravren aren't people."

His voice quieted as he stared down at the water, arms wrapped around his knees.

"The first time I saw one, I was sixteen. I'd never been in a battle—just the occasional fight on a border patrol. I was standing in the citadel when one of them tore through the walls. I couldn't believe my eyes. It was like something out of a nightmare."

He tensed at the memory, then grew very still.

"When it jumped at me, I froze. Aurelia jumped in between us... it took her head off."

Katerina's mouth fell open, but she had no breath to gasp. For a fleeting moment, she was absolutely certain she must have misheard. But a single look at his face confirmed it.

"Cass..."

What could you say? What could you possibly say to that?

He didn't expect a reply. He wasn't looking for sympathy. Only absolution.

"And last night, I froze again."

With nauseating horror, she remembered the look on his face. The childlike terror that had rooted him to the spot. Pale skin and enormous dark eyes. It was easy to imagine what he must have looked like at sixteen, staring at the monster that had just broken into his home.

"You were just a kid..."

He gave her a look that made her feel very young. *Just a kid* didn't cut it in the immortal world, even if at some point it technically applied. They lived by a different set of rules.

She tried a different tack.

"I'm sure she wouldn't have blamed..." His shoulders tensed and she proceeded cautiously, speaking in a quiet, demure voice. "You said yourself she never did anything she didn't want to do. Cass, look at you now. Look at everything you've achieved. She would be so proud—"

His hand flew up for silence. "I cannot speak of it."

"We don't have to speak," she said quickly. It wasn't often their roles were reversed, that she would be comforting him. She was determined to do a fantastic job. "We can just sit here—"

"That's not what I..." He trailed off, raking his hair back in frustration. "Please, can you just...can you just say something normal?"

She paused. "...something normal?"

Their eyes met.

"Anything."

She paused again, thinking. "Dylan's angry with me."

The fae's lips twitched. He stared at her speculatively, then his eyes flickered down to the perfect set of teeth marks on the inside of her wrist. "For that?"

She nodded, but Cassiel instantly disagreed.

"He wouldn't get angry for that. You saved Aidan's life, didn't you?"

She bit her lip; how did one explain it? "Yes, but it wasn't just... it was a *lot* of blood this time, and..." Words failed her as she gazed out towards the river. "Things... escalated."

He stared at her a moment, then looked away.

"That happens with vampires."

So factual. So blunt. When the reality was exactly the opposite.

"Has it ever happened to you?" she asked curiously. When they'd first met, she would never have dreamt of asking the intimidating fae such a personal question. She'd been nervous enough speaking to him at all. But things had changed. "Have you ever exchanged blood with a vampire?"

His eyes flashed to hers in surprise, trying to gauge whether or not she was serious. When he saw that she was, he actually laughed—getting to his feet before offering her a helping hand. "Princess, you still have a lot to learn."

She shot him a glare as they headed back to the others. "...you were a lot less condescending when you were dead."

BY THE TIME THEY MADE their way back through the trees, the rest of the friends were starting to wake up. Serafina and Kailas were tenderly, if painfully, intertwined. Tanya sat up quickly, only to bring a trembling hand to the gash on her head. Cassiel went to her immediately, while Katerina set out to find Dylan. As usual, he was keeping watch. Standing on a bluff with his eyes on the castle.

"It looks so peaceful from here," he murmured. "You'd never know anything happened."

She followed his gaze, hesitated a moment, then wrapped her arms around his waist, resting her chin on his shoulder. "Who could have made such a powerful curse? Even Alwyn never—"

"I don't know," he interrupted softly.

She paused, suddenly wondering how much his shifter senses had been able to overhear.

"But surely only a sorcerer could—"

"I don't know," he said again before turning to face her.

The long night had left bruise-like shadows beneath his eyes, shadows that were all the more striking in the bright afternoon light, and the hours of battle had most certainly taken their toll.

The shoulder he'd been throwing against the cell in the dungeon was completely crushed. Lines of dark discoloration snaked out from beneath the tattered remains of his shirt, up to his neck. At one point, he'd been bitten. The skin on his collarbone was torn with it, and Katerina shuddered to imagine whatever monster had been strong enough to get him on his back.

He was tired, sore, battered, and without the slightest idea as to why any of it had happened.

And yet... he was smiling.

"You look so beautiful in the morning."

She blinked, staring back at him in quiet amazement. Why was it that every person she'd met since leaving the castle all those months ago were always saying the very last things she expected to hear? Why couldn't they ever, just once, do something predictable?

Dylan was the worst one.

"It's...it's not morning," she stammered, cheeks burning with an unexpected blush as she tucked a strand of tangled hair behind her ear. "Don't rangers know how to read the sun?"

He smiled again, thrilled as always with her teasing. But instead of playing along, as he usually did, he simply pulled her into the circle of his arms. Carefully—as she was also hurt.

"I keep thinking I'm going to lose you, I keep finding myself in situations where something threatens to take you away... but here you are."

He kissed her softly, lips lingering on hers.

"Beautiful."

At this point, the young queen thought there was a good chance her head might simply explode. Between the sheer weight of everything she'd seen in the castle and now this sun-soaked declaration of love, the whiplash had left her thoroughly senseless.

She stared up at him, feeling unexpectedly shy. Then balked at his next words.

"I'm not upset with you."

A shiver of ice-cold dread froze her suddenly still. The warm glow of his affection vanished just as suddenly and she found herself holding her breath, desperately searching his eyes.

"You...you were listening—"

There was a sudden noise on the drawbridge and both of them glanced over, momentarily distracted, as Aidan and Petra emerged from view. One looked thoughtful, while the other looked grim. Neither was a particularly comforting reaction, given what they'd just seen.

Katerina stared at them for a moment before turning back to Dylan. She didn't know how or exactly why, but she suddenly believed with all her heart it was crucial to get this moment right.

"Dylan, I—"

He silenced her with a swift kiss, taking her hand in the same moment.

"Come on." He cocked his head toward the trees. "Let's get back to the others."

She nodded hastily, but her feet refused to move. "In a second, I just—"

He was already moving them over the grass, in a sudden hurry to reach the forest grove. "We need to figure out what to do next. Petra will tell us. Petra will know."

Her feet dug hard into the dirt as she pulled against him. "Dylan, will you just..."

He turned around slowly and she trailed into silence.

It wasn't the muscular cut of his body or the strong line of his jaw. It wasn't that blend of rugged yet ethereal features, or the way his lashes shadowed down his face. It wasn't the glow of his golden skin or the tiny dimple that hid at the corner of his lips.

It was his eyes. Those enchanting, sunlit eyes staring straight back at her.

"I'm not upset."

She stared at him a moment, utterly bereft of speech, then nodded her head.

No. He was furious.

Chapter 6

"It was a curse." Petra spoke with no preamble. A commander at heart, she required no introduction. She simply gazed down upon the bewildered, bedraggled friends, her sharp eyes studying each one. "But by whose conjuring and to what end...I have no idea."

Katerina stared at her a moment, then quickly lowered her eyes. It seemed like forever ago that she and the general had spoken privately, sitting beneath a tarp in a rebel camp. The strange woman had talked about her pendant, reminisced about her mother—Adelaide Gray.

Of course it's a curse. What else could it be?

Aidan met her eyes for the briefest of moments.

"You'd be surprised," he said softly. "There were several other possibilities and a curse was the least of them—trust me. We got lucky."

Katerina looked at him, thinking *lucky* to be a strange way to describe what had happened to them last night. What those other possibilities were, he never said. But maybe it was for the—

Wait a second—did he just READ my MIND?!

Aidan glanced at her quickly, then shook his head. Then he paled and looked away.

SEVEN HELLS!

"That's a powerful curse," Dylan murmured, his eyes lost in thought.

"And specific," Serafina added. "As far as I could tell, none of the beasts were interested in attacking anyone who was already frozen in the castle. It was like they weren't even there."

"Lucky them," Tanya muttered with a scowl.

The few hours of rest had given the friends a chance to catch their breath, but not much else. It had been a long night. And those wounds they'd suffered would not be quick to heal.

Of course, some of them had been healed already.

"Then why send them?" Aidan asked quietly, an almost apologetically perfect portrait of health. "The leaders of the five kingdoms were frozen. At their mercy. Why send an army of dark creatures, if they meant them no harm?"

There was a moment of silence, then Cassiel lifted his head.

"Because they didn't come for the people. They came for something else." His bright eyes sparked as they travelled from person to person. "When Katerina and I went to the upper levels, we found a Kaelar. It was searching for something—tearing the room apart."

"Searching for what?" Tanya twisted around in his arms. "The Kaelar are supposed to be scavengers. And not for things you'd find in a castle."

Katerina's eyes widened in dark curiosity as Serafina bowed her head with a sigh.

"The Kaelar are also supposed to be extinct."

There was a moment of silence, then Petra patted down a lock of the fae's tangled hair with a sympathetic smile. "Ah, child, but you've learned better than that by now, haven't you?"

She was perhaps the only person in the world who would refer to either Serafina or her brother as a child. Yet they both turned to her with the same pair of dark, entreating eyes.

"What should we do?" Cass asked softly. "It has been hundreds of years since I've seen beasts like that roaming the world. I cannot imagine an evil so terrible as to bring them back now."

Petra stared back at them steadily, widening her gaze to include the whole group. As many hundreds of years as the fae had been alive, she had been alive much longer. Long enough to see not only creatures such as those but the far older, far deadlier, creatures that had come before.

It was a matter of survival. But all hope was not yet lost.

"In order to find out who awakened them, you must find what they were searching for," she answered calmly. "That is the key to finding the answers you seek."

The others turned to each other with the same blank expression, but Katerina's chest tightened with a feeling of sudden dread. The creature hadn't been searching in the throne room or the treasury; he'd been in her private chamber. Going through her drawers.

"Guys..."

"It can't be a matter of tribute," Cassiel murmured. "The spell holds captive the ruling council of each of the five kingdoms. Any one of them could be ransomed back to their people for more than whatever might happen to be in the castle vault."

"Documents, then?" Tanya asked quizzically. "Plans outlining the treaty? We're in the middle of a peace summit to unite the entire realm. It would be damn coincidental timing for that and whatever's happening now *not* to be connected."

"Guys?"

"But there *are* no concrete plans," Dylan argued. "No battle strategies, supply lines—nothing that could be of use. The plan is simply to make peace. And, given the level of commitment we've seen thus far, I highly doubt anyone bothered to write that down."

"What about blackmail?" Serafina inserted quietly. "Something to give one of the kingdoms leverage over another. Some secret they threaten to expose."

"Like what?" Kailas turned to her with a sad smile. "The Damaris prince did some very *bad* things while the others were away?" An almost wistful expression came over him as he shook his head. "I wish those terrible things were secret, but they're not. I'd rule out blackmail. But we—"

"*Guys!*"

Katerina dug into her pocket, pulling out a tiny chest. The same chest that she'd rescued from her bedroom just a few hours before. Like it had a life of its own the bronze hinges sprang apart, spilling a cluster of sparkling rings into her open hands.

The gang caught their breath. But it wasn't the rings that made them nervous.

It was the tiny paper that fluttered out after.

"What's this?" Petra caught it between the tips of her fingers, turning it over with a very peculiar expression before she started to read.

'Five kingdoms to stand through the flood
United by marriage, united by blood
Protected through grace, as only one can
To take up the crown, either woman or man'

A sudden chill came over the sunny little clearing. The night of horrors had come to an end, but the friends found themselves suddenly more afraid than they'd been at any point during the endless battle. By the time Petra's low voice trailed off into silence Katerina was willing to bet any of them would gladly trade another hour or so in the castle, just to make that stupid chest disappear.

But there was no fighting it. And they were suddenly convinced.

This is the reason for the curse. This is what they were searching for.
...but why?

Petra froze very still, then brought up a hand to rub her eyes.

"I was very much afraid of that."

The others looked at each other nervously, while Dylan slumped down in the grass with a wearied sigh. "I told you we should have put it back."

"LET ME TELL YOU A STORY..."

Like school children gathered for a lesson, the seven friends settled around Petra on the grass. Unnaturally quiet and still. Heads tilted back at she paced beneath the afternoon sun.

"Many ages ago, when the world was still new and untamed, a prophecy was made about five unique individuals. Five individuals who represented each of the five kingdoms. Shifter, man, Kreo, vampire, and Fae. Five individuals who had the ability to rise above the bloodlines and kingdoms that divided them and bring about a new era of peace. In many ways, the world then was much as it is now. Awash with chaos. Ravaged by war. Above all things, it hungered for peace."

Her voice fell into a quiet rhythm, carrying the friends along.

"The five who had been chosen were delighted. Having shared in many adventures, they were already fast friends and took up the challenge with both hands. The five kingdoms fell in line behind them, and for many years they ruled in perfect harmony. For many years, all was well."

There was a hitch in her step.

"But such things are never meant to last."

The sky itself seemed to darken as her eyes lifted to the horizon, gazing into worlds the rest of them would never know, clouding with troubles long since passed.

The same troubles that had recently fallen upon their very doorstep.

"As time went on, the king of men grew increasingly unsatisfied. Not content with just his own kingdom, he wished to rule them all. Unite the realm under a single flag—the High Kingdom, he called it. The same kingdom we're sitting in now. What started as a private quarrel escalated into all-out war. The friends were divided. The peace between the five kingdoms fell apart. And in the madness and bloodshed that followed...the prophecy meant to unite them was lost."

Katerina was frozen on the grass, not even daring to pull in a full breath.

Sitting beneath the warm sun, she found herself imagining a cold night. One where the castle that stood so serenely across the river was under attack. Fire rained down from the skies, and the distant chorus of a hundred screams echoed through the forest.

Somewhere deep in the castle, in the darkness of an unlit corridor, a cloaked figure was pulling back a portrait. Its eyes sparked in the darkness as it hid the prophecy carefully inside.

Not lost...but saved. Hidden in secret for hundreds and hundreds of years.

Until the pendant led us right to it.

"So...what happened?" Dylan asked cautiously.

His eyes were lit with the same curiosity as the rest, and Katerina thought how strange it was they hadn't heard this story before. Then she remembered whose kingdom had defeated the rest in the war that followed. Coincidentally, it was the same kingdom that wrote the history books.

The Damaris legacy strikes again.

She and Kailas shared an uncomfortable look before turning back to Petra. The woman was staring at them all with a peculiar expression. Perhaps thinking how strange a combination was sitting before her. How unlikely the bonds of friendship that had managed to unite.

"The realm was in chaos," she replied simply. "It was the beginning of the First War."

"To the *people*," Serafina pressed, just as morbidly entranced as the rest. "What happened to the five *people* the prophecy had selected?"

There was a moment of silence, then Petra seemed to make up her mind.

"The fae was killed in a woodland realm, fighting against the king who'd betrayed them. The vampire drifted away to a wretched land where she named herself queen. The shifter shut himself away high on a mountain, forsaking the rest of the world, taking in all those unfortunates who were also lost. And the Kreo? She dedicated herself to a life of rebellion. Organizing camps. Rallying the defenseless. Endlessly trying to restore the fragile peace that was promised so long ago..."

The barest trace of a smile lit the hollows of her face.

"...only to wake up one morning and see history repeating itself. Only to discover that the age-old prophecy had fallen upon the shoulders of someone new."

The friends blinked up at her in silence, too stunned to move.

No, it can't be. It's impossible.

Michael. Petra. The Carpathian Queen.

Jazper...Dylan said her name was Jazper.

"What happened to the king of men?"

Katerina was just as surprised as the others to hear herself asking the question. However, despite the wave of raw panic building up inside her, it was suddenly the only answer she needed to know.

Petra stared at her for a long moment, then bowed her head.

"The man faded away into shadow, bound for centuries with ancient magic. Cursed to remain in the place of his greatest betrayal... only recently to have been released."

...only recently to have been released.

There was a loud ringing in Katerina's ears. Her skin was pale and tingling. Like something out of a dream, she remembered Cassiel's words as they wandered through Laurelwood Forest all those months ago. The tragic battle that marked the end of his people. The Fae queen's dying spell.

'The Red Knight had won the day, but he would not live to see another.'

What if the queen had meant the words literally? Not that the man would die, but that he would never be able to move forward. Forever cursed to relive that fateful day.

Then the other part of the story clicked into place.

'And if a child of man were ever to again set foot in the forest...he would not leave it alive.'

Her heart stopped beating. The ringing suddenly stopped.

"But we left..." she whispered in horror. "We left... and it broke the curse."

The fae from the prophecy was Queen Eliea herself. And the king of men? The one whose betrayal had ripped the five kingdoms apart? It was none other than the Red Knight.

And we set him free.

Her eyes drifted up to the castle like she was seeing it for the first time. All those shadows inside, the nightmarish creatures that roamed within? That was their fault. An ancient darkness was spilling like poison into the land, and they had no one to blame but themselves.

"That's impossible," Tanya whispered, but it sounded like she was trying desperately to believe her own words. "The Red Knight—"

"No one ever found out what happened to him," Kailas murmured in a hush. "He and his entire army...they just never came back. They were never seen again after that day."

"The Red Knight." Petra made a strange noise, one that could have been laughter but had long ago darkened to something else. "I'd forgotten people used to call him that. I always knew him by another name. Nathaniel Fell."

But how is that possible? My father was king during the rebellions. A Damaris king. Did the man simply never age—like Petra, and Jazper, and Michael? Did he never have any heirs to pass on the family name?

"And Eliea?" Cassiel asked with quiet dread. "You're saying that..."

He trailed off, unable to finish. The final wish of a dying queen, a beloved leader of his people, and they'd torn the ancient magic apart. All they'd had to do was survive.

Petra softened with genuine sympathy, laying a hand upon his shoulder. "Yes, child. Your dear aunt did all she could to defeat him. And for many, many years he was contained."

Dylan's head jerked up as Tanya tensed with a start.

Cassiel's aunt? He'd certainly failed to mention that!

Not that it mattered. The damage was done. Only the horrible lesson remained.

Some curses were never meant to be broken.

The little clearing was abruptly silent. No one had any idea what to say. No one had any idea what to do. As they sat there, bleeding quietly on the grass, they found themselves so caught up in stories of the past that they failed to realize how it connected to the present. How five new people had been chosen. How the prophecy of old had fallen upon the shoulders of someone new.

Petra watched them for another moment, giving them a chance to work it out. When it became clear that wasn't going to happen, she decided to give a gentle nudge.

"Michael would be proud."

Dylan lifted his head, staring up at her in a daze. "...what?"

Her face tightened, but she forced a smile. "He cares for you like a son, took you under his wing." Her head cocked to the side as she considered it. "Perhaps he always knew you would be the one to replace him. The shifter to take up the call. My brother always had a strange way of intuiting those sorts of things..."

Dylan froze for a moment, then pulled away with an involuntary shudder. If Petra was trying to be comforting, the words had the opposite effect. The mere mention of his old mentor was enough to send a visible tremor through the ranger's body, paling his skin to a sickly shade of white.

"...proud?" His eyes dilated in horror as he gazed at the castle. "We *freed* the man."

"As it was always meant to be." Petra knelt into his line of sight. "Eliea would have been the first to tell you, an evil so great cannot be contained. It must always be defeated—"

"And Michael!" Dylan sprang to his feet, barely hearing her words. "We asked him about the prophecy the day before the attack. We asked him if it was real. He said he knew nothing about it!"

Petra pursed her lips, thinking it poor form to smile. "And Michael would be the first to tell you these things must be worked out in their own time. You cannot simple be told the answers—"

"But you're telling us now," Tanya said angrily, pushing to her feet. "And I for one think it's total *bullsh*—!"

"Tanya," Cassiel chided softly, but his heart wasn't in it.

"No—this is ridiculous!" she insisted.

The light of the battle was still glowing in her eyes, coming only too soon after the last time they'd put down their blades. If there was a burden to be shouldered, an ancient prophecy to be fulfilled...she wanted no part of it.

"This was *your* failure. *Your* generation's mess." She stared at the ancient general without a trace of fear. "*You* need to clean it up."

"Tanya," Cassiel warned again, sharper this time.

"What?" She flashed him a scathing glare as he pushed gingerly to his feet. "The prophecy was made about *them*, not us—she said it herself! For all we know, they're still the ones who are supposed to fix it."

"They're not," the fae said tiredly, rubbing his eyes.

"How do you know?" she insisted defiantly. "They're certainly more capable than the likes of us. You saw what she did to those trolls, you remember the Carpathian Queen. Be honest, who would you rather have defending you—Michael or Dylan? No offense," she added distractedly.

The ranger shot her a sideways glance, but didn't disagree. There were few people in the world he trusted and respected more than Michael. He'd certainly trust him to save it.

"The prophecy isn't about them, because there aren't five of them left!" Cassiel cried, his temper finally getting the better of them. "My aunt is dead. Their covenant is broken."

A heavy silence followed his words. A silence none of them could escape.

"He's right," Petra finally murmured, staring at Tanya with a look of unmistakable pity. "I'm so sorry. I wish it wasn't so. Such a burden should not be placed on someone so young. But the five of you were drawn to each other, united against all odds. A Fae working with a Damaris. A priestess of the Kreo, with a vampire and a Hale. As if that wasn't enough... you found the very prophecy."

None of the others could meet her gaze. They were lost to their thoughts. Only Kailas and Serafina glanced at the rest, looking desperately apologetic and profoundly relieved at the same time.

"United through marriage, united through blood..."

Cassiel spoke softly, then lifted his eyes to Petra. He didn't ask the question directly, but it hovered between them all the same. She stared only a moment, oddly hesitant to meet his gaze.

"Michael and I were siblings," she replied softly, "a blood bond. And at some point, I'm sure Jazper sank her teeth into all of us."

It was a good effort, but it was impossible to lie to a Fae.

"United through marriage," he said again, staring intently into her eyes.

She stared a moment longer, then her shoulders fell with a sigh. Whatever the answer, she had wanted to spare him. But it clearly wasn't meant to be.

"Eliea and Nathaniel were in love," she said quietly. "They had no idea how it would work, of course. An immortal Fae and a mortal man. We didn't know then what we know now."

Cassiel's eyes flickered instinctively to Tanya, then a sudden question creased his brow. "What do you know—"

"They loved each other so deeply," Petra mused, her memory drifting back through time. "I couldn't believe it when he..." She flinched. A woman who'd led the rebel armies for hundreds of years *flinched* at the thought. "Michael and I both felt it... when he slid the sword through her back."

Cassiel's lips parted, then he suddenly walked away. Standing with his back to the rest of them on the bank of the river. She stared after him for a moment before turning to the rest.

They hadn't progressed much in their thoughts.

"I can't believe it," Dylan murmured, staring off into space. "I can't believe that we triggered this. That we were the ones to set him free. It was my idea to go into the woods..."

"Don't do that," Petra said firmly. "The prophecy had yet to be fulfilled. That means the curse was always meant to be broken. Look now to the future; do not dwell on the past."

Alwyn knew.

Katerina was sitting very still, arms wrapped protectively around her chest.

She remembered the wizard's cryptic words back in the dungeon, when she'd heard the lilting words of the prophecy for the first time. He'd known exactly what was going on, chided them for assuming it was a mere coincidence that such an unlikely group had ended up together.

"What does that mean?" Tanya interjected sharply. "Look now to the future? Why do you people always have to speak in riddles? What *exactly* are we supposed to do?"

The contrast couldn't have been any greater. The towering commander with a thousand years of experience versus the tiny shape-shifter, grass stains on her knees and a look of raw adolescent defiance in her eyes. And yet something about them was undeniably similar.

And yet... the prophecy had chosen them both.

"Tanya Oberon." Petra's lips twitched up with the hint of a smile. "What you must do is very simple. You and your friends must fulfill the prophecy, where myself and the others could not. You must unite the five kingdoms and defeat the ancient darkness spilling into this land."

...doesn't sound very simple.

"But we were working on that," Dylan murmured, still speaking in a sort of daze. "We were gathering everyone together—"

"But we hadn't counted on the Red Knight," Katerina interrupted, eyes flickering to the high stone walls. "Which begs the question: What was he looking for in the castle?"

The man already knew the prophecy—he didn't need to find it. And having already stabbed his immortal beloved in the back, it wasn't like he was in desperate need of those diamond rings.

It was quiet for a moment, then Petra lifted her head.

"He was looking for the amulet."

The friends looked at her in surprise as Katerina lifted a hand to the jewel. Since getting it back from Aidan after the battle, there hadn't been a single moment that it hadn't hung around her neck. Dylan sometimes complained about it when it burned at inopportune times.

"...the amulet?"

'Protected through grace, as only one can.'

Alwyn had wanted the amulet, too. He'd gone to great lengths to acquire it, following her into the Kreo jungle for another chance to rip it off her neck. He'd known about its potential to protect—he'd known a lot better than Katerina, who'd yet to understand how that part of it worked.

"He wants it for protection?" Serafina asked curiously. She and her brother may have arrived late to the party, but they'd made sure the others had caught them up. "But does he really need it?"

It was a depressing observation, even more so because it was true. The man had overcome the councils of the five kingdoms with a single curse. So assured was he of his eventual victory, that he hadn't even ordered his creatures to destroy them—assumedly preferring to do it himself.

He did all that without setting a foot in the door. Does he really need the amulet?

"Ah, child... it isn't the amulet that gives protection. It's merely the stone." Petra held out her hand and the necklace lifted into the air, the gold chain straining against Katerina's neck. "And the stone itself was never meant for a pendant. It was to be fitted into a crown."

'To take up the crown, either woman or man.'

"A crown?" Dylan repeated, looking blank. "What crown?"

"One that was forged in the old kingdom, long ago," Petra answered softly. "One that will give him complete invincibility should he ever acquire it, should he ever unite it with the stone."

The friends shared a look before Tanya went out on a limb.

"Well, do you happen to *have* it?"

Petra threw back her head with an unexpected laugh. One that Katerina thought was entirely inappropriate, given the direness of their situation. One that made the seven friends jump as they stared back at her, still dripping tiny streams of blood onto the grass.

"Oh child, if only it were that simple." Her eyes twinkled as she gazed down at her shell-shocked audience. "Before going our separate ways, the three of us who remained hid the crown somewhere we knew Nathaniel would never find it. The one place we knew it would be safe."

Katerina was unaware such a place existed. She would have moved there long ago. "Where?"

The friends stared at Petra in a kind of daze. Holding only one piece of the puzzle. Desperate to find the other before it was too late. By now, they should have guessed the inevitable answer.

"Taviel."

Chapter 7

Katerina stood a bit away from the rest of the group, watching as Petra said a private goodbye to each one in turn. She hadn't been brave enough yet to ask exactly where Taviel might be, but she gathered from the looks on their faces that it was quite a journey.

Travelling alone in the wilderness while a flood of darkness sweeps into the land.

Great.

"—keep sending me off on suicide missions with these people," Aidan murmured, smiling faintly when his mentor laughed. "At any rate, I don't see why it has to be me. You should have heard Alwyn back in the dungeon. The prophecy could easily have been about any vampire."

Petra stared down at him fondly. "But you and I both know that it could not have been just *any* vampire," she countered with a secret smile. "You and I both know it takes a special kind of vampire just to *show up.*"

Katerina didn't exactly understand her implication, but Aidan's face went pale.

"I don't know what you're..." At first, he tried to deny it. Then he realized it was useless and hung his head. "I'm sorry."

Her eyes twinkled as she lifted his chin, staring deep into those luminous eyes. "It isn't me who deserves your apology. Trust works both ways, Aidan. You've asked these people to trust you. It's time you start trusting them in return."

He sighed quietly, then nodded—vanishing from sight as Cassiel and Dylan walked forward side by side. Petra opened her arms wide, embracing each of them.

"My boys."

They bowed their heads with matching smiles as she bent to kiss their cheeks.

"Be safe, be strong—in that order." It was a maternal command, but a command all the same. "If news reaches me that either one of you has been harmed, I'll resurrect you myself just to kill you all over again. Is that understood?"

Dylan grinned down at the grass, having heard such a command many times before. "Yes, ma'am."

Cassiel was a little more hesitant. The ranger drifted away, but he froze where he stood, a truly devastating expression on his face. "I promised myself... I promised I'd never go back."

Over five hundred years, and the fae had never gone home. Katerina realized with a start that, like most of his people, he didn't have a home to go back to.

Petra stared at him for a moment, then chose her next words with deliberate care. "I heard they gave you a Lithian Heron."

Just a passing comment, but it was somehow enough. Cassiel lifted his head in surprise, then his beautiful face warmed with the hint of a genuine smile. "Yes, they did."

Without another word, he was off to help Dylan—raiding the commander's provisions as they prepared to depart. Kailas was already there, unwinding a roll of bandages for Serafina, and so caught up in his task that he didn't notice the pair of onyx eyes fixed on his face.

"Serafina, do you need—"

"*Kailas Damaris.*"

The young prince froze as Petra swept towards him, reaching out a silent hand.

The woman had just used the same hand to crush the life from a pair of trolls. The same woman had recently raised a rebel army to end his life. Now she was reaching for his face.

Serafina tried to move between them, much the same way Dylan had stood in front of Katerina at Pora—earning him a giant sword to the throat. But Cassiel was suddenly there, holding her back. Perhaps he was placing his faith in Petra. Perhaps he was hoping she'd do away with the prince after all.

Either way, it was out of his hands. Or any of their hands for that matter.

The clearing seemed to hold its breath as the two stared at each other. The ancient rebel commander, and the teenage Damaris prince.

It was quiet for a long moment, then Petra flicked his cheek with a smile.

"...you have glass in your hair."

It was like popping a balloon. The group let out a deflating sigh of relief as Kailas dropped his eyes quickly to the ground, running a trembling hand through his hair. Sure enough, several pieces of broken glass showered to the ground. Petra smiled again before moving on to Serafina.

"Well, that's one way to introduce yourself," Dylan murmured, wrapping his arm without seeming to think about it around his girlfriend's waist. Katerina nodded.

She wasn't entirely convinced Petra wasn't trying to kill him after all. She'd seen her twin brother in many impossible situations, but right now he looked on the verge of a heart attack. She studied them for a second more, then cast a tentative glance at the ranger's arm.

So he was speaking to her then. And cuddling with her. And in light of this new adventure that had befallen them, he seemed determined to act as though everything was fine.

But she remembered the look in his eyes. That murderous spark when he'd smiled and told her that he wasn't upset. She was willing to bet Aidan remembered it, too.

"Hey, are we..." She twisted cautiously around, chancing a worried look at those impossibly blue eyes. "You and me, we're—"

Then Cassiel called softly and the ranger turned his head. A second later, he pressed a swift kiss on her forehead before heading off to help the fae once more.

"We're fine."

She stared after him, feeling a part of herself grow heavier with each departing step.

...right.

"Dear child, you look as though the world's about to end." Her mournful trance broke and Katerina lifted her head to see Petra watching her with a little smile. "It hasn't. At least, not yet."

The queen grinned in spite of herself, repeating a phrase Cassiel had used just a few hours before. "What is that—gallows humor?"

"The best kind there is," the commander answered. "It can keep you alive—that kind of perspective. Center you when it feels like everything else is spinning out of control..."

Katerina's cheeks colored with a blush. As usual, there wasn't a doubt in her mind that Petra was seeing more than she ought to. Intuiting things the queen wasn't fully aware of herself.

But as she stared up at her, tilting back her head in the sun, she suddenly found that she had a more pressing problem than the intemperate heart of one ranger.

Her problem was the ranger himself.

There wasn't a doubt in her mind that Dylan was the shifter in the prophecy. Everything in his life seemed to have led to that very point. His elevated birth, the tragic demise of his family, right down to his inexplicable tutelage by Michael—an alpine passing of the torch.

But therein lies the problem.

"Petra..." The queen stared shyly at her hands. Since those ruby wings erupted from her back, she'd been too frightened to ask anyone the question. It had plagued her day and night, but still, she was silent. Now she found herself opening up to one of the most intimidating people in the realm.

"I may carry the name of Damaris, but in blood I'm a Gray." Her bright eyes fixed on the general's face, searching for any hint of reaction. "I'm a shifter like my mother. The leader of men in the prophecy...it couldn't be me."

The words seemed to carry a physical weight. Pushing her forward, dragging her down.

A part of her was relieved to have said it. Relieved that she might have escaped that particular twist of fate. Another part was awash in such dejected sadness she thought it might lift her right off her feet.

To watch her band of friends go off without her—place themselves in mortal peril, united by a single unearthly cause? To watch them fulfill of prophecy of which she had no part?

She didn't think she could stand it.

"Kat, come on!" Tanya called, hoisting a bag over her shoulder. "It's time to go!"

The queen turned her head to see the lot of them standing beside the river. Looking very much the way she was used to seeing them before they'd returned and surrendered themselves to their gilded cage. Windswept and bloody, but with the same unexpected smile lighting their faces.

Dylan, in particular, looked like something out of a dream. The golden glow of the sunset lit up the sky like a halo behind him. Dancing in his eyes as he gazed restlessly at the horizon.

But how can I be meant to go with them? How is there a place for me there?

It was as if she'd spoken the question out loud. A throat cleared behind her and she turned, blushing, to see Petra watching her with that same knowing smile.

"Have faith, Katerina Damaris." Her eyes twinkled as she cocked her head towards the forest trail. "You should have learned by now... things are rarely what they seem."

THE PLAN WAS SIMPLE: get as far away from the castle as possible, then find a safe place to stay the night and tend to their wounds.

As far as plans went, it was remarkably short-sighted. Given the notoriously controlling ranger who'd come up with it, it was uncharacteristically vague. But for the life of them, none of the seven friends were physically able to muster up anything more.

It was a testament to the miserable state of their condition that Petra almost didn't allow them to go. (At first, Katerina thought such presumed authority quite silly. Then she took another look at the woman and stared obediently at her toes.) But like it or not, whether the realm was aware of it or not, the five kingdoms were under attack and the castle was nothing more than a battlefield.

They could not linger. They must make haste.

Even if some of them were having an easier time than others...

"Here, let me help you with that."

Aidan slid the pack off Serafina's shoulders and onto his own. It bumped and jostled against the other three bags he'd already confiscated. With Kat's blood running fresh through his veins, not only was he apologetically uninjured but he was slightly more effusive than usual.

"No, it's fine." Serafina tried to reclaim it, but her painful attempt was too slow for the vampire's fast hand. "You shouldn't have to—"

"I don't mind, really!"

He raked back his hair with quick, jittery fingers, his already-sparkling eyes almost cartoonishly bright, and every breathless word seemed to pour out of him in an uncontrollable rush.

"In fact, you really shouldn't be walking on that leg. I heard it snap when the two of you fell off the stairwell, and you know what they say about the dangers of unattended breaks. If you like, I can carry you. I mean, I don't have to or anything. But the offer's on the table. In fact..."

He shifted aside the bags with a look of sudden inspiration, "maybe you could just climb up on my back—"

Cassiel caught him by the shoulder. "What are you doing?"

The vampire lifted his eyes to see the entire group staring back at him, paused in various positions on the trail. He froze in his tracks, looking a little confused at the outburst himself. "I...I don't know."

Kailas studied him for a moment, the breathless chatter ringing in his ears, before his lips curved up in the ghost of a smile. One look at the vampire's face confirmed it, and he turned his head quickly to the side. Trying hard not to laugh. "You drank my sister's blood."

As if to reaffirm it, the vampire's face flushed a guilty shade of red. "Just...just a bit."

By now Tanya was openly laughing. Cassiel shot her a chiding look, but his own face had warmed with a secret smile. Only Dylan wasn't laughing. He acted like he couldn't hear.

"I'm guessing it was a little more than that," Kailas teased. "I'm guessing it was a *lot*."

Katerina blanched as Aidan flashed the prince a threatening look.

"...there's always room for more."

Kailas lifted his hands with a grin as his twin sister flashed him a look of sheer murder.

"I have a great idea," she said with false sweetness. "Why don't we talk about how you somehow failed to lock the cave trolls in the kitchen? Perhaps you forgot to close the door."

"I *did* close the door."

"Then how did they escape?"

He raised his eyebrows, all those years of separation and forced maturity breaking down in a common sibling brawl. "How did two *cave trolls* escape from the kitchen? I don't know, Katy. Maybe they asked something bigger and stronger for help. Wait a second... they're freakin' *cave trolls*."

"I'm just saying... it was your only job."

"Oh, come on!" He threw up his one working hand. "You can't possibly blame me for that!"

At this point Dylan let out a quiet sigh, circling back around. "You remember all those months you tried to have her killed?" he asked softly, taking the prince by the shoulder and steering the siblings apart. "Remember those royal infantrymen you sent to spear us alive?" The two men locked eyes. "Don't yell at your sister."

Katerina folded her arms with a smirk, but it faded as the ranger walked past her.

"...he's not wrong," he whispered loud enough for Katerina to hear.

The group was suspiciously quiet for the rest of the day.

THEY WERE HOPING TO get a lot farther than they did. They stopped miles short of their original goal. However, with the exception of the vampire, the friends were simply unable to continue.

"*Seven hells,*" Cassiel cursed through gritted teeth, lowering himself painfully onto the grass. A series of deep punctures was bleeding freely down his leg. Punctures that looked suspiciously canine in nature. "The next time you shift, I'm turning you into a coat."

Dylan turned immediately, but for once he had no sarcastic reply. He'd yet to recover his balance after mauling his best friend. He'd yet to take in a full breath after seeing him die. "I'm sorry," he murmured, sinking down beside him. "What can I do?"

The fae shot him a look, then fished a dagger from his belt and pressed it into the ranger's hand. "Wedge this between your ribs, then roll down the hill. It'll make me feel much better."

Dylan's lips curved obediently at the joke, but his eyes stayed fixed on the bloodied leg. At any rate, he certainly looked ready to do it. If only to ease his friend's suffering just a little.

"Cass, I..."

This time Cassiel stopped what he was doing, registering the change in tone.

"What is it? What's wrong?"

Katerina stared between them, catching her breath.

Were they so desensitized? Could the fae not even fathom what might have his young friend upset enough to stay still, to hold his tongue? Do I really want to be so jaded? One of the prophesized ones?

Dylan took a second to steady himself. Just a second. Then he flipped up the knife with a little grin. "How about I just cut it off instead? We could find you a lovely prosthetic."

Katerina stepped back into the shadows, blinking free of her trance.

Gallows humor. Right.

As the two men got to work, slowly tending to their wounds, she wandered a bit away from the rest of the camp. Not long ago, Dylan would never have let her do it. Not long ago, he forced a light-hearted interrogation just to keep her talking while she stole a forbidden bath.

But things had changed. Around the time she started shooting fire out of her hands and changing into a dragon, he decided she was probably safe to wander on her own.

Only a few moments of walking through the trees she saw through to the other side, to a lovely little farmhouse, nestled in the grassy clearing. Accustomed as she was to the fineries of the castle, it seemed almost painfully picturesque. Brick walls strewn with ivy, wildflowers swaying softly beneath the windows, a spiraling curl of smoke coming up from the chimney.

She thought, for a fleeting moment, she might actually prefer such a peaceful existence. She thought, for a fleeting moment, that she could imagine herself and Dylan living in such a place.

Then she realized she wasn't alone.

"Sorry," Aidan said quietly. "Didn't mean to startle you."

He was standing in the trees just a few feet away, hands in his pockets as he stared down at the farmhouse as well. The soft glow of moonlight clung to the smooth contours of his skin, and the backdrop of stars made him look like some kind of heavenly prince surveying his earthly kingdom.

Or maybe that's the blood.

"I've been doing that a lot today," he sighed, speaking before she could answer. "Talking before I thought out what I'd like to say. It's most unnerving."

She bit down on her lip as he shot her a sideways smile.

"I suppose you're so used to it by now, you hardly notice."

This time just biting wasn't enough, and the queen threw back her head with a sparkling laugh. "So now you know how it feels to be a teenage girl. You're welcome."

He shook his head, grinning in spite of himself. "My wildest dream come true."

They stood there in silence for a while, staring down at the farm, mulling over the events of the day. It seemed that each one was stranger than the last. From the death of the delegates to the strange curse that had overtaken them in the woods, right down to the trolls beating down the doors of the castle. But momentum like that seemed to ebb and flow.

One moment they were fighting. Now they were staring at a quiet farm.

"How are they doing back there?" He caught her curious stare and rolled his eyes. "I thought it was probably best to excuse myself until more of this gets out of my system."

She laughed again, quieter this time. With a secret blush. "They'll be fine." The carefree banter echoed back through her mind, and her brow creased with a little frown. "I don't think they'd allow themselves to be otherwise."

Aidan shot her a quick look, but didn't disagree. His eyes returned to the farm.

"It seems so pointless," she muttered under her breath. "That they wouldn't just take your blood to heal. It wouldn't be like the two of us. It's not like they..."

She trailed off suddenly, alarmed by what she'd been about to say. Again, the vampire stared at her. This time he seemed unwilling to remove his gaze.

"Blood isn't simple, Majesty." His voice was light, but the words carried a weight she was only beginning to understand. "It always comes with a price. It must be one you're willing to pay."

Their eyes met for a split second, then they turned to the clearing.

A price you're willing to pay...

"Aidan... when Cass was hurt before, you wouldn't use your blood to revive him. He was dying, but you still refused. You said a vampire and a Fae couldn't share blood."

"No, never."

He was a lot less rude than Cassiel, but answered with just as much certainty. When he saw her look of confusion, he tried to explain. "You must have thought it very callous, but vampires and Fae are on the opposite ends of the spectrum. Giving my blood to someone like Cassiel wouldn't be the same as giving it to you."

Katerina stared in open confusion, trying to understand. "Opposite ends of the spectrum?"

Aidan nodded slowly. "Creatures of darkness, and creatures of light."

She absorbed that for a moment, pondering the mental toll it must take to refer to oneself as a 'creature of darkness.' Making a mental note to discover where on the spectrum she fell. "So, what—your blood would kill him?"

"No, it wouldn't kill him. But it wouldn't heal him either." Aidan's face grew thoughtful as he stared out at the farm. "I imagine it would make him very sick."

The queen nodded slowly, unable to look away. "And his blood... it would do the same to you?"

"No." He bowed his head suddenly, hiding the look on his face. "Quite the opposite."

She took another second to absorb this before suddenly shifting gears. "Who do you think lives down there?"

He shrugged. "An old couple. They're sleeping downstairs. I debated..." He trailed off, unwilling to finish the sentence. "They're fast asleep."

"Do you really think Petra keeps sending you off on suicide missions?"

He let out a laugh, unable to control it. The layers of tension between them vanished as he shot her a rueful grin. "You're a *nightmare* with questions. It's no wonder the others can't stand me."

Katerina grinned shamelessly, refusing to back down. "Do you think she keeps sending you away?"

"Yes."

"Do you mind?"

"Yes."

"Do you *really* mind?"

There was a pause.

"No."

She didn't think so. At the same time, it was often impossible to guess whatever was going through the vampire's head. Most of the time, she was simply winging it.

The breeze picked up and she wrapped her arms around herself with a sigh. "Just another memorable day in the High Kingdom..."

He made a compulsive move towards her, then dug his hands deep into his coat. "You're the one who was so desperate to get back that damn crown."

Yes, she was. And now they were after another.

Try as she might, she couldn't wrap her head around it. The whispered words of an ancient prophecy. Kingdoms rising and falling like the swelling of the tide.

They had been brought together—she and her friends. Without ever being aware of it, before they were even born. Tanya and Petra. Cassiel and his aunt. Dylan and Michael. Aidan and Jazper.

Me and Nathaniel Fell.

"Dylan's angry with me," she said softly, surprising herself with the words. It was one thing to say them to Cassiel, who might be able to help. It was another entirely to say them to Aidan.

He lifted his dark eyes to her for only a moment before his shoulders fell with a sigh. "He isn't angry with you, he's angry with me."

"For what?" Katerina snorted humorlessly. "Almost dying?"

"You said it yourself—it isn't something they allow."

She tried to force a smile, but ended up shaking her head. "You didn't hear him say it. You didn't see the look on his face."

"But I felt it." The vampire hung his head, dark hair blowing into his eyes. "He isn't angry with either of us... he's just angry."

The quiet words seemed to echo between them, making Katerina more desperate with every pass to make them go away. "But nothing happened! It wasn't like we were actually—"

Aidan silenced her with a single look.

"Katerina... he's right to be angry."

Chapter 8

The decision was made to not go any further. The decision was also made to not terrify the poor old farm couple by showing up bloodied on their doorstep in the middle of the night.

They would do it in the morning. Manners first.

Instead, they prepared to hunker down for the night—laying out a saddle blanket as they settled down on the grass. It was highly uncomfortable. It was highly cold. But unless Katerina was imagining it she could swear the others were enjoying it *just* a little, like she was herself.

The sound of the wind whispering through the trees. Breathing in the open air.

Everything was so closed off at the castle. So protocolled and aloof. Katerina had once witnessed a royal breakfast where none of the participants were allowed to speak, just because the duke who'd assembled them had incidentally forgotten to greet them as they sat down. Instead of rectifying the situation, instead of acknowledging the absurdity and moving on, they proceeded to eat in perfect silence. Not even looking at each other as they sipped daintily at royal Champagne.

It's not like that out here.

Katerina grinned again as Tanya gave the blanket a sharp tug, leaving the rest of them bare and exposed. Dylan's hair was tangled in her own. She was sharing Serafina's scarf for warmth.

They were all sleeping soundly except one. The vampire who'd volunteered to keep watch.

Morning came before anyone would have liked, blanketing them with a layer of frost. It woke them with a chill, and it wasn't long before Katerina found herself staring up into a pair of beautiful blue eyes. A second later, she found herself yelling the vilest profanity she had ever heard.

This is SO MUCH WORSE the day after!

"Yeah," Dylan laughed softly, "that's kind of how we feel."

Her entire body was wrecked. Head to toe, there wasn't an inch that was spared. For lack of better description, each injury felt very much like the thing that had caused it. She had plunged to her death off a stairwell. She'd been tossed into a wall by a cave troll.

And she'd hardly gotten the worst of it.

Serafina's leg had been rendered virtually useless—the stiffness that had set in overnight made it impossible to bend. The deep gouges in Kailas' shoulder were in a similar state, and while the prince was trying his best to be brave a sickly pallor had set in around the edges of his skin.

Tanya wasn't sitting at all, but was propped up against the base of a nearby tree. Cassiel was attending her as best he could, but every inch of his flesh was still bearing testimony to both the battle in the castle and the wolf attack that had happened just a few hours before.

And her beloved Dylan, whilst forcing a smile, was as broken as Katerina had ever seen. It was the way he was holding himself. Like he was trying very hard not to scream.

"I'm going to shift." He reached out to tuck back a curl of her hair, then gritted his teeth in agony and lowered the hand back to his side. "Just for an hour or so. Just to heal. Then I'll track us down some food and we can decide what to do next."

She nodded silently, wincing over the fractured bones in her wrist. "In the meantime, we could take cover in that farmhouse."

"...what farmhouse?"

There was a sudden pause as the two stared at each other.

She'd almost forgotten that he didn't know. The fearless ranger had been so exhausted he'd fallen asleep on the spot. She shifted guiltily then forced herself still, reminding herself with even breaths that there was nothing to feel guilty about.

"Aidan and I found it last night." She gestured over his shoulder, feeling the weight of those piercing eyes. "It's in a clearing just through those trees."

There was a beat of silence. Then he pushed suddenly to his feet. "Yeah... I'll check out the farm-house."

The raw edge in his voice tore at her heart. There was so much going on behind those beautiful, troubled eyes. So much that he was unwilling to say.

"Dylan—"

But he was already gone. The man vanished and shifted into a wolf so fast, he barely had time to shed his clothes. She stared after him for a moment, then walked slowly through the trees, picking them up, one by one, placing them in a pile for him just outside the view of the camp.

All that was left to do was wait.

The hour passed by slowly, much more slowly than any hour should. Having Cassiel as a protector at the castle had shielded the young queen from most of the injury levelled her way, so she quickly dedicated herself to helping the others get back on their feet.

Again—not the easiest task.

"What the heck do you think you're doing?!" Tanya pulled back with a furious shriek as Katerina pressed a cloth soaked in whiskey to a laceration on her arm. The sting must have been incredible but, strangely enough, that's not what had the shape-shifter so upset. "CASS!"

The fae appeared out of nowhere, lifting the two girls apart like they weighed nothing more than dolls. "What is it?" His dark eyes rested first on Tanya, who was seething like Katerina had just murdered her dog, before turning to the queen. "...Kat?"

"Nothing," she breathed incredulously, holding up the cloth. "I was just disinfecting it—"

"—with the *whiskey*!" Tanya cried. "She was disinfecting it with our *only* flask of whiskey!"

The fae blinked in surprise as Katerina lowered the cloth slowly into her lap. They both stared at it for a moment before she lifted her head with a tentative, "...really?"

"It's the only flask!"

Without another word she snatched it from the queen's dainty hands, taking a long swig before giving it to her boyfriend for safe-keeping. "Honestly, Kat...we try to look out for you, try to teach you the ways of the wild...but *this*? It's like you're *deliberately* trying to antagonize me."

"Wouldn't want that..." Katerina muttered.

Without another word she slipped discreetly out of reach, listening as the shape-shifter continued venting to the fae. She left them to it, joining her brother and Serafina by the fire where a very similar process was happening. Only, instead of using alcohol, the fae was using a flame.

"I'm so sorry, my love," she whispered, pulling his arm taut as she heated the metal edge of a blade in the fire. "But it's the only way to stop the bleeding."

And it certainly was bleeding—*profusely*. Just four geometric gashes in his shoulder but the fabric was soaking with it, while the prince himself had turned a dangerous shade of pale.

"I know," Kailas said quickly, though the mere act of holding the limb straight was clearly testing his limits. "It's fine. Do what you have to."

Katerina froze the moment she sat down, staring with wide, horror-stricken eyes. She had seen the royal doctor do this only once on a poor infantryman who was injured away from the castle and the rest of his tools. The blunt cauterization had burned into her mind, as had the young man's screams. She'd thought about them both many times since.

"Wait, can't you...can't you stitch it or something?"

She didn't want to break their momentum, she didn't want to make her brother—who was trying to be so brave—lose heart. But she didn't want to hear him scream like that either.

Serafina gave her a sharp look, while Kailas paled a deeper shade of white.

"I have no needle or thread," the fae said quietly. "And these were made by a Naket, so they won't heal on their own. We have to do something to stop the bleeding."

Katerina didn't know what a Naket was, and she didn't want to ask. All she knew for sure was that she couldn't let her twin brother be burned by something as blunt as a heated blade.

"Then let me."

The couple turned to her with matching looks of astonishment.

"Vengeful much?" Kailas' eyes flickered between his sister and the blade, wishing there was more distance between them. "You were the one who said we were fine—"

"That's not what I meant!" Katerina interrupted quickly, appalled by his misconception. "It's just that I can do it with a little more precision... if you'd let me."

They stared at her blankly until she raised a slender hand. A cluster of flames leapt from the top before quickly cooling—leaving her fingertips an iridescent red.

There was a moment of silence. Then each one cried out at the same time.

"That's perfect!"

"Absolutely not!"

They turned to each other, both glaring at the other's stubbornness.

"Kailas, see reason," Serafina chided. "It's the best way and you know it. She'll be able to do a much better job than I could with a blade—I don't know why I didn't think of it myself."

Because it's grotesque and cruel?

Kailas seemed to agree.

"See *reason*? You're asking me to let my twin sister melt my skin back together with her bare hands." He shuddered involuntarily, freeing his arm. "I'd rather just cut it off—no offense, Katy."

She lifted her hands innocently, letting them work it out.

"Would you?" Serafina challenged calmly. Her delicate eyebrows lifted into clouds of white hair, fixing him with a look that could shame a priest. "Would you rather just cut it off? Because that's certainly what it's going to come to if you don't let this happen."

Katerina dropped her eyes to the ground, feeling intensely sorry for him. Not just for the wound, but for the chastisement. She had learned the hard way never to argue with a Fae.

"It'll be quick," she offered hesitantly, flexing her fingers inside her sleeves to keep up the heat. "Just a few strokes—then it's all over."

Serafina flashed her a quick smile, then nodded encouragingly at Kailas—as if the thought should be much more palatable now. When that didn't work, she raised her voice innocently and called across the clearing for her brother.

"Cass, can you come here? I need your help with a little knife-work."

That did the trick.

Faced with the prospect of either his twin sister or his girlfriend's militant older brother, Kailas chose the option less likely to result in his death. With a look of supreme hesitation he offered out his arm to Katerina, watching her warily all the while. "Have you..." He cleared his throat, trying his best to control the tremors shaking his voice. "Have you done something like this before?"

She wrapped her fingers carefully around his wrist, trying to ignore the torrent of blood that followed, trying to ignore the way his skin trembled beneath her touch.

"Oh, yeah. About a dozen times," she said easily, flexing her fingers again until they were glowing with the heat of a thousand flames. "It's actually how Dylan and I met. He was bleeding like crazy from a halberd to the chest... I cauterized it in about four seconds flat. Saved his life."

There was a pause.

"...I know how Dylan and you met."

The siblings locked eyes. Then deliberately looked away.

"Just trying to be reassuring."

"You're not."

"Preferably *before* he bleeds out on the forest floor..." Serafina suggested casually.

"Right." Katerina rubbed her fingers together, then tightened her grip on his wrist. He tensed automatically against her, then made a visible effort to hold still. "On four, you ready?"

His eyes flashed up, bright with fear.

"Why on—Shit!"

He let out a tortured cry as her fingers pressed into his bare shoulder, melding the skin back together, sealing the wound shut. In a morbid sort of way, it was a bit like painting—smoothing pale lines of flesh within a swirling sea of crimson, wiping any imperfections away.

Finger painting!

...he'll appreciate that when he's not screaming.

The first cut was the easiest. The second two required a bit more work. By the time she got to the last one, both Serafina and Aidan were holding him steady as he writhed and thrashed.

One was weeping quietly. The other was staring at the blood.

"Okay!" She pulled back quickly, lifting her hands into the air. "That's it. I'm done!"

The prince slumped forward, clutching weakly at his ravaged skin, while the others held him steady as best they could—looking both impressed and slightly sick. For a while, no one knew what to do. The only sound was the whisper of the wind in the trees and the prince's ragged breathing.

Then a sudden gasp made them lift their heads in surprise.

In hindsight, it must have looked rather strange.

Katerina—her hands dripping with blood. Kailas—being forcibly held down by the others.

Cassiel and Tanya were standing at the mouth of the clearing, staring at the scene with expressions of perfect shock. To Katerina's surprise Dylan was right behind them, freezing in his tracks the second he saw the bound and bloodied prince.

For a second, no one said anything. Then Cassiel's eyes flashed up in rage.

"Why didn't you *wait* for me?!"

Dylan's eyes snapped shut as Serafina rose to her feet, looking as dangerous as Katerina had ever seen. Keeping her eyes locked on her brother the whole time she pulled the heated blade from the coals of the fire, rotating it slowly in her hand.

At this point, the fae seemed to realize his mistake. "I just mean... I could have helped. Helped *heal* him," he emphasized quickly. "That's all."

Seven hells.

Kailas jerked away from the vampire's supportive arms, leaning shakily against the base of a tree. The ground was literally soaked with blood, and Aidan pulled in a quick breath before crossing deliberately to the other side of the clearing, putting the fire between himself and the prince.

"What about you?" Katerina asked Dylan, breaking his attentive gaze. "You're back a lot sooner than I thought."

"I heard the screaming," he answered quietly, tearing his eyes away from the burns on Kailas' chest and looking at his girlfriend's fingers instead. "I also scoped out that farmhouse and I think it's a good idea. If the owners are amenable, we can stay the night there. Just judging by the looks of things, we could all use a bit more time before heading out on our own."

As he was talking Tanya pulled herself out of Cassiel's arms and shuffled painfully across the forest floor, sinking down beside the fallen prince as if he was something to be studied.

"Geez... that's disgusting." She resisted the urge of poke at it when she caught his scathing glare. "I mean, I'm sure it's going to heal up nicely. Good work, Kat."

Aidan rolled his eyes, taking care to keep his eyes from the bulk of the blood. "He probably could have just done it himself, if what I saw in the ballroom was any indication."

The others looked at him in surprise before turning to the prince with the same expression.

It was true. They hadn't had the wits to talk about it yet, but all of them remembered quite clearly the moment when Kailas had let loose a wave of devastating fire—scorching the Carpathian lion in the dungeon. He'd used the same fire to take down the Kasi in the ballroom upstairs. By all accounts he probably could have sealed the wounds, if he'd only thought of it himself.

And that's not all he could do...

Katerina fell back a step, staring at her brother like she'd never seen him before. She doubted he'd put it together, she doubted the rest of them had put it together as well, but a sudden thought fell heavy upon her shoulders. Once it settled, it was unlikely to ever leave.

I'm not the only monarch in the High Kingdom. I'm not even the only dragon.

...what if the prophecy is about Kailas instead?

Chapter 9

When Katerina was six years old, her governess had taken her on a rare outing to the local village. They'd gone in disguise, of course, accompanied by guards who were equally disguised, and the young princess watched with wide-eyed wonder as the peasant children put on silly hats and costumes and ran from house to house—knocking on the door, asking for sweets.

It was the Festival of Carnassas. An ancient celebration wherein the villagers feasted and danced and sang, sharing in the bounties of the harvest and beckoning in the new year.

She remembered watching in fascination as hordes of screaming children ran up and down the streets, candies and sugared fruit smeared upon their lips. Growing up with the strict protocols of the castle, she remembered being shocked by the simple audacity of knocking on a stranger's door. Expecting them to welcome you into their house and give you things you didn't deserve.

This felt very much the same.

"Good morning!"

The door to the farmhouse pulled back to reveal an elderly woman—a woman whose mouth fell open in shock when she saw the people standing on the other side.

"What in tarnation...?"

They had tried to be strategic. Only a few standing on the porch (the girls), and a few of the more volatile-looking candidates (the vampire and the renegade prince) standing farther back.

Those precautions seemed rather silly now.

"Good morning," Serafina said again, smiling sweetly.

It had been unanimously voted that the Fae princess should be the one to speak. As if her angelic, trustworthy features weren't enough, she was one of the only members of the group whose clothes had somehow not been stained with an incriminating layer of blood.

"I'm so sorry to trouble you," she continued politely, "but my friends and I have found ourselves in a rather strange—"

"Good heavens!" the old woman gasped. "You're all covered in blood!"

The friends shared a quick glance, but no sooner had the fae pulled in a breath to try again than the old woman was calling at the top of her lungs for her husband.

"Richard!" she cried. "Richard, come quick!"

There was a creaking in the floorboards above them; the friends shifted nervously on the porch. A second later, an elderly man was hobbling slowly down the stairs.

"Really, woman? If you don't stop your yammering—" He stopped cold when he saw the collection of battered teenagers at his door. "Well, I'll be..."

It was a gamble as to whether or not he recognized them. People who lived in the outer villages seldom visited the capital, and even if he had it wasn't like he was going to run into any of the young monarchs walking on the street. Although the legends and lore had been filled with many colorful descriptions, most commoners wouldn't be able to recognize their own sovereign.

Even if that very sovereign was to show up at their door.

"Please, sir, pardon the intrusion." Serafina's lilting voice eased the tension as she offered the man a lovely smile. "I know it to be an odd request, but my friends and I have been travelling for many miles and were wondering if there was a way we could shelter here for the night. We're prepared to pay you handsomely..."

As if on cue, a delicate bracelet of white diamonds slid off her wrist. Kailas shot her a fleeting glance, and Katerina wondered if it had been a gift.

The couple didn't register the jewels. They were too busy staring at the people.

"Have you ever seen such a thing in your life?" the woman mused aloud, fingertips lacing over her mouth. "Because I have *never* seen—"

"Where are you kids headed?" Richard interrupted curiously.

The man might have been old, but he was a good deal sharper than his age had led Katerina to believe and he had seen more of the world than his wife. Already, there was a flash of intuition as he studied their faces, one at a time. A knowing twinkle that could work either for or against them.

It was Dylan who answered, lowering his eyes respectfully. A ranger, not a king. "We were taking the northern trail up to Cazrat when our caravan was attacked by Esos raiders." The man might rule a kingdom on the other side of the realm, but he was shockingly up to date on local rivalries. "Most of us managed to get away, but—"

He froze as the woman grabbed hold of his shirt.

"Richard, they're hurt!"

An astute observation.

The man's mustache twitched with the hint of a smile. "Yes, dear. I can see that." His eyes leveled on the young king, who shifted uncomfortably under his gaze. For a moment, he seemed to be considering. "Esos raiders, huh?"

Dylan didn't miss a beat. "Yes, sir."

He had been well-trained to lie, but his eyes stayed down. He was unable to hide the monstrous tears in his skin and clothing. And there was something a bit too familiar about his face.

Luckily, the old man was as curious as he was kind. "You just need a place to wait out the night?"

"Just one night," Serafina assured him swiftly. Her brother gave her a discreet nudge and she stepped forward—all enormous eyes and quivering lips. "I promise we won't be any trouble."

She was good. *Shockingly* good. It made Katerina wonder if it was an encore performance. If the fae and her brother had to beg for the charity of strangers when they'd been children on the run.

The couple glanced at each other only a moment, then the woman opened her arms wide.

"Of course you can stay! Come here, child. Let's take a look at you!"

Child, again.

Katerina glanced with secret amusement at both of the Fae, wondering if it ever got old. If it did, they certainly didn't let on. Serafina stepped forward with perfect obedience. Only someone who knew her well could see the slight hesitation as she surrendered herself to the fussing hands of the old woman. The slight stiffening to her limbs as she allowed herself to be embraced.

"Poor dear," the woman murmured, wiping a smear of blood from the fae's face as she silently marveled at her long white hair. "Attacked by raiders, she's already too thin—"

"Helen, why don't you get our guests some food from the cellar?" Richard suggested smoothly. Perhaps he could see the fae's discomfort after all. "I'll get them settled in down here."

By now she had essentially adopted Serafina in her mind, but she nodded quickly—hurrying down the corridor with a series of whimpers and frantic sounds the others could hear long after.

Her husband smiled fondly, then beckoned the group inside. "Well come on in, then. Don't let Helen scare you."

With instinctual caution, the gang followed him through the door. The house was as simple as they expected, but there was an odd sort of comfort in that. A reassurance in things being small, being close by. None of the high ceilings and shadowy corridors of the castle.

They proceeded through a well-used parlor then out through the kitchen, into the sunny yard that ran along the side of the house. Katerina wondered if he'd brought them there on purpose. If he'd sensed the trauma and claustrophobia and tempered it with the compromise of a fenced lawn.

"You all right?" he asked gruffly as Dylan struggled to take off his cloak.

"Fine." The ranger manhandled his fractured shoulder, shoving it through the fabric with a wince. "Thank you for this. I'm not sure if we could have done another night in the woods."

Richard nodded slowly, eyes taking in even the smallest detail. "I'm surprised you didn't just shift."

The entire party stopped dead still. Dylan looked up slowly, meeting his gaze. "...excuse me?"

The man lifted his shoulder in an innocent shrug. "That helps your kind heal, doesn't it?"

Dylan opened his mouth to answer then stood there in silence, looking a little overwhelmed. "I don't..."

He trailed off, wondering if it was worth it. The man had clearly guessed for certain, and yet shifters still found themselves faced with a level of discrimination—especially in the High Kingdom.

"Peace, Sire." The man clapped a soft hand on his uninjured shoulder. "It's hardly the worst of your secrets. Though I'd implore you not to tell my wife. She's quite... excitable, as you've seen."

Dylan's lips parted in shock, then curved with a grateful smile. "Of course. And... thank you." Their eyes met. "Truly. We appreciate it."

The man smiled warmly, pleased that it was all out in the open. "I was a trader for Lord Harris back in my youth; travelled all over the five kingdoms, saw all sorts of different people." His eyes flickered over the group, glowing with pride. "I knew who you were the moment I saw you. And them? I've never seen one in person, but I know they're Fae."

Katerina shot Cassiel a nervous look, but to her extreme relief he didn't roll his eyes. He simply inclined his head with a gracious smile. But the revelations weren't stopping there.

"We gathered days ago in the town square to celebrate the summit," he continued quickly, suddenly in a rush to get it all out before his wife returned. "A special prayer was said in the hopes that all would go well. Of course, we haven't heard anything since..."

And then we show up bloodied at your door.

For the first time, his eyes turned to Katerina—the queen of his own kingdom. It was only after that she realized he'd been avoiding her on purpose, too overcome to look upon her directly.

A strange sense of calm washed over her and she found herself lifting his chin, knowing instinctively all the right things to say as she gazed steadily into his eyes.

"You and your wife did well to pray," she said quietly. "And you did well to invite us in. You have my word—your kindness will not go unrewarded."

The man looked on the verge of tears.

"No reward is necessary, Your Majesty." He bowed his head respectfully, white wisps of hair blowing across his forehead as he stared at the ground. "You honor us by your visit. It is a true privilege to aid you and your friends in whatever way you require."

This time, it was Katerina who was overcome. Months upon months, she'd been forced to listen to poetic litanies of praise from those who'd come to serve her at the castle. Not one of them had moved her so much as this man's simple words in the garden of his woodland home.

"Of course... I'd still prefer if we didn't tell my wife."

The queen released him with a burst of sparkling laughter, warming to him through and through. Behind her the others were watching with quiet smiles, feeling very much the same. "It will be our secret."

A clumsy crash echoed from somewhere inside and he shook his head with a faint grin. "Helen will be making her famous rabbit stew—I beg your forgiveness in advance." He gestured to the house with a brisk nod. "We have rooms upstairs enough for all of the ladies and another two rooms in the back of the house. I'm afraid it's not enough for everyone..."

There was a meaningful pause as his eyes flickered involuntarily to the infamous prince and the vampire. Kailas froze uncertainly, but the vampire's lips twitched up in a crooked grin.

"Perhaps the two of us could sleep in the barn..."

KATERINA HAD THOUGHT it was a joke, but that night the men in question actually went outside to sleep amongst the bales of hay. The old couple was as sweet as they come, but even they didn't have the stomach to allow a vampire to sleep on the couch—let alone Kailas Damaris.

Dylan quite graciously offered to join them in solidarity, while Cassiel refused outright and said he preferred to stay indoors.

The queen watched from the upstairs window as they made their way slowly across the lawn, casting long shadows in the grass. Kailas was slightly affronted, Dylan couldn't have cared less, and Aidan was so used to such treatment he hardly would have noticed if it weren't for the quiet remonstrations of the prince. *Those* he found to be quite amusing.

"Cheer up, Your Highness," he said with uncharacteristic brightness. "We'll make a stable boy out of you yet."

Dylan chuckled softly, whilst Kailas shot them both a dark look.

"It isn't the barn," he insisted, "it's that they don't trust me to sleep indoors. They think I'll go crazy and murder them all before morning."

...not completely unwarranted.

"Well, look on the bright side," the vampire continued earnestly. "Now the only people who have to worry about that are us."

There was a pause as Kailas looked at him before his lips curved up in a reluctant smile. "It really is like you're channeling her..."

Aidan's own grin melted right off his face as the prince vanished inside the barn, feeling significantly better about his night—leaving an awkward silence in his wake. The vampire sighed deeply but was about to follow, when Dylan reached out suddenly and grabbed his arm.

"Can we talk?"

...oh crap.

Even though they couldn't see her, Katerina crouched down beneath the windowsill—barely breathing, trying to slow the frantic pace of her heart. Her friends happened to be quite distracted at the moment, what with the impending homicide, but if either one was paying the least bit of attention they'd certainly be able to hear.

Aidan froze in the darkness, then tilted his head nervously towards the barn. "We should probably get inside..." He and the ranger shared a memorable look before he dropped his gaze to the ground. "Or yeah, we could talk..."

The queen peeked over the sill; only her eyes were visible. They had a hard time making out anything in the darkness, but she could have sworn she saw the vampire blush.

"Listen," Dylan began softly, "it isn't what you think—"

"I'm sorry!" Aidan blurted. All of his signature grace and poise vanished into a tangle of raw nerves and emotions. "I never would have asked her to do it if there was literally any option left. As it stood, I still thought it was a bad idea. I know what you're going to say and I'm so sorry, Dylan. If you can just forgive me—"

He cut off suddenly as Dylan held up a silencing hand. The two men stared at each other for a long moment before the ranger's lips twitched into the most unlikely smile.

"The only reason you're apologizing is because it's what Katerina would do."

Aidan paused a second, thrown off course. "That's not true—"

"Yes, it is." Dylan's face was still lit with that same peculiar smile. "If it wasn't for her blood, you would never."

The vampire shifted uncomfortably, then stifled a sigh. It seemed the two men had danced around the subject long enough. Despite his best efforts to avoid it, the game was up.

"She's very... emotional. It's difficult."

Okay, I'm not THAT emotional—

"How was it with me?" Dylan asked curiously.

Katerina dug her fingernails into the wood, leaning closer. She remembered quite clearly the night her boyfriend had volunteered to share his blood. Coincidentally, it was the same night she'd almost had her hand chewed off by a giant panther. He'd instructed the vampire to take whatever he needed to heal and, like it or not, their relationship hadn't been the same since.

"It was difficult," Aidan admitted. "In other ways."

"Like what?"

"Massive savior complex, the instinct to devour raw birds..."

Dylan gave him a playful shove, then grew serious. "She did it to save your life, Aidan. I don't want you to die—you *know* that." He lapsed into silence, staring intently into the dark. "But that's the only reason she did it."

Aidan froze for a moment, then nodded slowly.

The two men walked inside.

"Hey, creeper."

Katerina slipped to the floor with a gasp, clutching weakly at her chest. Tanya was standing behind her with a wide grin, a pile of unused towels and blankets in her arms.

"Your *Royal Majesty*," she chided teasingly, "we weren't eavesdropping, were we?"

"What—no!"

It would have sounded a lot more convincing if she wasn't still crumpled in a pile on the floor. With as much dignity as she could muster Katerina pushed stiffly to her feet, trying her very best to avoid the shape-shifter's impish gaze.

"The Hempers are certainly kind, but you're doing their laundry now?"

Right after their talk in the backyard, the seven friends had proceeded to experience the full array of country hospitality. They had been bathed, fed, bandaged, and pampered. Even the more standoffish members of their group (the men she'd been spying on) found themselves indulging in a secret grin as Helen fussed and coddled—squeezing over seventy years of maternal instinct all into one eventful night. After they'd cleaned up, there was stew. After stew, there was cobbler. After the cobbler, there was a series of well-intentioned, probing questions by the fireside as she ran a comb through every lock of Katerina's long hair.

What was their business up in Cazrat?
Were they getting enough to eat with the caravan?
Would they like her to go after the raiders herself?

She was hopelessly endearing, touching that deeply-buried part in each of them that had always desired such unconditional affection, though their own mothers had long since passed away.

By the time they headed up to bed, Tanya was seriously considering kidnapping them both.

The smile slid off her face as she glanced down at the bedding in her arms.

"No, I was just going to offer you an extra blanket and find out if your wrist was feeling better." With a look of sour satisfaction she flung a quilt at the queen's head, reveling in the flinch that followed. "Nope. Looks like it still hurts."

Katerina glared at the back of her departing head. "Always good seeing you."

"'Night, princess."

As the door clicked shut she rotated the quilt slowly, wincing as little stabs of pain radiated up her arm. It was true, her wrist wasn't any better than the moment she'd fractured it. Not that surprising, considering it had happened only a few nights before, except that the others were already well on their way to recovery. The vampire only needed blood, the Fae healed at a much faster rate than humans, and the cuts and bruises were already fast-fading memories on the shifters.

She stared at the discolored skin with a slight frown, an uneasy feeling gnawing away in the pit of her stomach. *As a shifter myself...shouldn't this be healing, too?*

It was a bloody good question. If she'd been thinking clearly, it was perhaps the only question that really mattered. But she had no time for it. There were other issues that required her attention.

Other people she needed to see.

Just one hand in front of the other...

As quietly as possible, the young queen hoisted herself out the window and began the precarious climb down to the yard. She could have just used the stairs but that would have risked waking Cassiel, and she didn't want to answer the fae's inconveniently perceptive questions right now. She had quite a different target in mind and she planned on being the one asking the questions.

If I can just get down this trellis...

It always looked so much easier when other people did it. She had seen Dylan scale walls and climb down buildings a hundred times.

Come on, princess.

Great, now she'd abandoned the title as well.

You can shoot fire out of your hands. Broken wrist or not, you can climb down a farmhouse—

"Running away, are we?"

With a stifled shriek, she lost her grip entirely. The trellis disappeared and the next second she was falling backwards into the open air... landing lightly in a pair of strong arms.

"I don't blame you—what with our chances." Dylan caught her without the slightest bit of effort, continuing his thought as if she hadn't just dropped down from the sky. "But I can't begin to tell you how it devastates morale when our fearless leader tries to sneak away in the night."

Katerina blushed, her arms wrapping automatically around his neck. How many times had he carried her like this? Her head resting against his shoulder. Her legs draped lightly over his arm.

"...or when she falls out her own window."

Another blush. This time, she braved a look at his face. "Dylan, I—"

"You can't do that again."

She froze in his arms, caught off guard by the sudden change in tone. For a second, her eyes drifted back to her room in the farmhouse. "With the window—"

"Katerina... you can't do that again."

Apparently, I'm not the only one looking for some kind of resolution.

He set her down on the grass. The two of them stared at each other in the dark.

Finally, when the silence could go on no longer, Katerina broke it. Albeit, with a voice about half the volume as the one she would have liked.

"He was going to die, Dylan."

"I understand that, and I'm not saying..." He lowered his eyes, pulling in a slow breath. "I care about Aidan. I would do anything I could to save him. It's just... you *can't* do that again."

"What are you—"

"Anyone else, Katerina." There was a quiet plea to his voice, one he didn't seem aware of himself. "Anyone else can do it. I'd have shifted back myself."

She shook her head. Knowing he was right, knowing she was right. Grasping at straws.

"You've given him a lot more blood than I ever have—"

"But I've never had his. It isn't the same." He ran his hands through his hair in a quiet sort of panic. "Kat, I know you mean well, but I don't think you understand exactly what..."

But she did understand. That was the problem.

She knew exactly what was happening when the vampire lowered her slowly onto the ground, stretching out to lie on top of her. She recognized the heat in her own body, the raw animalistic impulse when the two of them locked eyes.

But when that's weighed against his life?

"What would you have had me do?" she asked quietly.

He stared at her for a long moment, then tilted back his head with a sigh.

"Nothing. You did exactly as I expected you to." Her eyes filled with hurt and he shook his head quickly. "I only meant... you saved his life."

It was quiet for a long time.

Then without another word, he kissed her on the forehead and gathered her up in his arms. A second later, he was scaling the wall in just two easy jumps—depositing her gently on the bedroom floor while he perched in the open frame.

He watched quietly as she took a second to catch her breath. Watched as she gave him a shy smile, a shy kiss, then tiptoed through the darkness into bed. She'd all but shut her eyes when he called out quietly once more, unable to stop himself.

"Katerina... just don't do it again. Ever."

Chapter 10

Katerina opened her eyes the next morning to the smell of bacon wafting up the stairs. She stretched a little, wincing against the bright sunlight, then cradled her throbbing wrist.

Definitely not better. Definitely not getting better.
Just broken.

She pulled herself out of bed with a quiet sigh, wondering when the whole 'silver-lining' part of being a shifter was going to kick in. The flying around and occasional bursts of fire were all well and good, but the unparalleled senses? The ability to supernaturally heal?

Her friends had counselled her to be patient, guessing that the abilities had lain dormant for so long they would need longer to awaken. But by now even they were starting to wonder.

There was a rattling of silverware and she hastened to get dressed.

The Hempers had proven generous in more ways than one. Not only had they provided food and shelter for the night, but Richard had promised to take the friends into the village that morning as well. He claimed to have business in town and offered everyone a ride in the back of his cart.

Katerina speculated the 'business' could have waited any day.

She was also starting to agree with Tanya's idea of kidnapping.

"Guys, you awake?" she called as she passed Serafina and Tanya's closed bedroom doors.

There was no answer and she quickened her steps down the stairs.

The last thing she wanted to do was be the last one down to the table. During her time in the wilderness, she had learned the hard way the benefits of punctuality. Cassiel had taken great pleasure in teaching her one day, by making sure the pots and pans were already cleaned and put away by the time she opened her eyes and stumbled out of the tent for breakfast.

That day, they had hiked forty miles. She was never late again.

"Good morning!" she called as she rounded the corner, sliding a bit on the smooth floor.

Not late at all, she thought smugly. *Only Helen and Richard are already awake.*

She flashed them a bright smile, giving the smoking bacon a cursory poke before pulling out the nearest chair. "Actually, do you guys want me to take that off the stove? It's burning."

There was nothing but silence. Coils of smoke drifted in from the kitchen.

"Richard?" She put a hand on his shoulder, hovering behind his chair. "Do you want—"

He fell face-first onto the table. Landing on his empty plate.

It was only then she saw the ashy pallor of their skin. It was only then she noticed the glassy eyes. And it was only when he fell forward that she saw the gleaming knife sticking out of his back.

Katerina let out a deafening scream.

"Kat!"

Dylan was there before the sound could echo into silence, sliding to a stop as she had on the hardwood floor. His face paled when he saw the lifeless couple, but before he could take a single step a shadowy figure appeared behind him and hurled his body up the stairs.

Katerina blinked after him. Unable to process what she'd just seen. "CASS!"

It was a knee-jerk reaction. One that had never failed her... until now.

There was a series of sounds from outside the window and Katerina whipped around to see a miniature battle taking place in the yard. The barn had emptied and Kailas, Aidan, and Cassiel were being swarmed by what looked like some kind of goblin horde. They may have stood at half their size, but there were dozens and they were lightning fast. No sooner had the men gotten hold of one of them than three more would spring up in their place. They were biting freely as well as lashing out with razor- sharp claws.

They were armed with the same knives used to kill Richard and Helen.

...holy crap!

Dylan was gone. The creature had taken off after him. The girls were missing, all other backup was otherwise engaged. There was only one thing left to do.

"Babe—I'm coming!"

In a flash Katerina was racing up the stairs, taking them three at a time. There was a thick trail of blood leading from the landing into the nearest bedroom. She stopped cold, then sprinted alongside it and kicked open the door. It banged against the wall as she froze in sudden fright.

Dylan was lying on the floor, barely breathing.

The monster was kneeling on top of him, slowly taking off his clothes.

...what the heck?!

Her face went blank. It was hard to make sense of what was happening.

Never before had she seen such a creature. It was huge, easily over ten feet tall, and shaped vaguely like a man. But a man that had no face. A man made entirely of shadows.

And those shadows had weight.

Dylan was trapped beneath it, fighting desperately but completely outmatched in terms of strength. To be fair, Katerina wasn't sure anything *could* match the thing in strength. It may have lacked the sheer size, but she felt suddenly certain it could overpower even a cave troll.

It was holding Dylan too tight to breathe, in too much pain to shift—needing only one hand to subdue him as the other ripped open the front of his shirt.

"Wh—" He tried to lift his head, but was slammed back by the heavy hand on his chest. The other continued rummaging through his clothes. "What are you—"

There was a sharp crack, followed by a cry of pain. Another of his ribs had broken. His body spasmed helplessly against the wood as a silent tear slipped down his face. He saw her a second later.

"Kat," he tried to gasp, but the thing was pressing him so tightly against the ground he was unable to pull in any air. "Kat—run!"

It was the lunacy of the words that brought her back to life.

Leave you here?! Are you bloody crazy?!

She lifted both trembling hands, trying her best to steady them as she let loose a wave of molten fire... except nothing happened. Not for the first time those intemperate flames failed her, stymied by the paralyzing fear pounding away inside her head.

Come on—don't do this to me! Not now!

Again and again, she tried. Again and again, she came up short.

"Kat, please! Get out of—"

Dylan broke off with another cry. This one sounded different than the first. Faint. Like he was calling out from somewhere very far away.

With a final surge of strength he grabbed fistfuls of the creature's ragged cloak, trying desperately to push it away. It hardly seemed to notice. It was groping around in his pockets now, tearing through the belt on his pants. Without seeming to think it leaned even closer, pressing him deeper into the wood. The floorboards splintered beneath his shoulders, sending up jagged spikes around his head. His face went pale and his entire body trembled—unable to withstand the weight.

It's going to asphyxiate him.

The creature didn't seem to care whether it killed him or not. At this point, she doubted it would even notice. It simply continued its deadly work, tearing off random pieces of clothing.

What can I do?

The fire wasn't working, that much was clear. And if the thing was able to overpower a guy like Dylan, realistically she didn't stand a chance. Waves of debilitating terror threatened to freeze her once more, but she dug her fingernails into her palms and forced herself steady. There was no time to panic; she had to be smart. Her only advantage was the element of surprise. If she was going to stop this thing, that was her best chance—

Then Dylan let out a heartbreaking cry and those logic centers shut down.

She broke a vase over its head.

Big mistake.

The creature turned slowly, tangles of the ranger's dark hair caught in its hands. Its eyes were the same as the Kasi—gaping black holes in the middle of its face. Sightless eyes, she realized. Like most other creatures from the hellish dimension, it was blind. But after a moment of moving its head back and forth, it stopped suddenly—zeroing in directly where she stood.

She was up against the wall a second later, fighting back a scream as the creature lifted her right off her feet—tearing open the front of her dress.

"*Kat!*"

Dylan tried to get up, then fell back down in the pile of broken floorboards. A violent shudder ripped through him and he coughed up a mouthful of blood. There was no second attempt.

The creature's hands were everywhere. Ripping through the fabric stretched across her bodice, effortlessly dangling her off the floor. She kicked frantically at its legs, but it made not a shred of difference. She felt her skin tear and blister beneath the impossible strength of its hands.

Then, all at once, it froze.

Its fingers curled around the delicate gold chain wrapped around her neck. The one that held up her mother's fiery pendant. The stone flashed in the air between them as the queen suddenly realized what the creature had been searching for all along.

To be invincible, you didn't just need the crown. You needed the amulet as well.

"No!" she screamed, yanking it back as the creature lifted its cloaked head.

For a moment, it seemed to be staring at her. Almost as if it had only just realized she was there. Then it pulled back its hand, preparing to knock the life out of her once and for all.

Her mouth fell open as the sounds of the battle faded away. Dylan's eyes were closed and he wasn't moving. For all she knew, he was already dead. As for the rest of them, they were too far away to help. They would defeat the goblins, or not, then come racing upstairs, only to find them.

One, asphyxiated on the floor. The other, a bloody memory painted across the wall.

And the amulet?

The amulet would be long gone.

Not like this. She stared in silent horror at the creature's hand, waiting at any moment for it to strike. *It can't end like this.*

The world around her stilled as she closed her eyes, pulled in a quiet breath. Then—

"NO!"

A cloud of fire engulfed the room, lighting up the darkness as the queen was thrown against the wall. There was a screeching wail as the creature stumbled backwards, thrashing violently, a pillar of flame. Just seconds later it dissolved into a smoking mess of shadow, writhing and twisting on the floor, fading away into absolute nothingness until only the fiery pendant was left.

And there was Kailas. Standing in the smoke.

His face was as pale as Katerina had ever seen it. Not an ounce of color to support the deep bruises or his over-dilated eyes. He took one look at the fallen amulet before stepping right over it and grabbing his twin sister, holding her in a crushing embrace as her feet swung over the floor.

She let out a quiet gasp, too stunned to speak. Digging her fingers into his shirt, burying her face in his waves of dark hair. He'd kept such a careful distance from her since the spell had lifted back at the castle, maintaining a strict barrier against physical contact.

She'd been grateful for it then. She was grateful for this now.

Then the world came crashing back into focus.

"Dylan!"

She pushed against her brother, streaking over the second her feet touched the floor.

His eyes were closed and he hadn't moved an inch since he'd fallen. There was a pulse but no breath sounds, and a frightening bluish tint had laced its way over the surface of his skin.

She reached him at the precise moment that Cassiel burst into the room.

One look at Dylan and it was Kerien all over again. The fae was back in the dungeon. Staring in helpless horror as one of his closest friends lay dead upon the floor.

He froze for a split second, then shook himself out of it and blurred to her side.

"What happened?!" he demanded, falling to his knees beside them. "Is he—"

"I don't know what it was," she whimpered, clutching the bare skin around her neck. It felt naked, violated somehow. In a way she was just beginning to understand. "It was like shadow..."

There was a distant shouting from the room next door. Kailas vanished the next instant, and the vampire streaked up the hall just a second behind. Cassiel stared after them, stricken with indecision.

"Did you find—"

"Tanya's here," came Aidan's swift reply. "They're both fine. We've got them."

Free from that extraordinary concern, the fae turned his attention to another. He made no mention of the ranger's disheveled clothes, aside from discreetly pulling up his torn pants. It was the breathing that held his focus. Or lack thereof.

"Like shadow..." he murmured back Katerina's words, running his hands skillfully up and down the ranger's skin. When he got to a specific point, he suddenly stopped. A second later, he pressed his ear to Dylan's chest. "His ribs collapsed. There's too much pressure on his lungs."

Katerina stared at him without blinking.

It seemed like only yesterday she was saying the same thing about Cassiel himself, after the avalanche when he was bleeding out in the snow. She'd saved his life that day. Given him her cloak.

The two locked eyes. She shook her head.

"I can't do it. My hands, they're shaking..."

Truth be told, she couldn't feel much of anything in her hands. The creature's grip had rendered the top half of her body completely numb. She was in absolutely no condition to be wielding a blade—let alone stabbing one into the chest of the man she loved.

Cassiel hesitated, glanced down at Dylan.

"I've never—" he started to say, then he shook his head and held out his open hand. "Give me your knife."

Does he really think I have a knife? That I wouldn't have used it by now?

Their eyes met again and he gestured impatiently. "A piece of glass—anything!"

"Here!" Kailas reappeared in the doorway, whipping a blade out of his belt and pressing it into the fae's hand. "Take mine."

Cassiel grabbed it without looking and in a single graceful movement, a movement that required shockingly little premeditated thought, he slid the blade into Dylan's ribcage.

The ranger let out a sharp cry, then went still.

"Now pull it out," Katerina instructed quietly. Her senses were starting to come back to her, faster now that she saw he was really alive. "*Slowly*... very slowly."

Cassiel did as he was told, deliberately slowing down as the blade slid out of his friend's body, slick with blood. For a second, nothing happened. Then he pressed softly on Dylan's chest.

"SEVEN HELLS!"

The ranger pulled in a gasping breath, only to let out a string of profanities. A second later he flipped onto his side, coughing up what looked like a small ocean of blood.

"It's okay," Katerina soothed quickly, propping him up as best she could and smoothing back his tangled hair. "It's okay—it's gone. Everything's going to be okay."

The fae was kneeling on his other side, murmuring softly in his native tongue.

There was more coughing. Dylan clearly wasn't taking in a word they said. His eyes were in constant danger of closing and he shook his head weakly, half-delirious with pain.

"That thing... it wanted..." He pulled in a ragged breath, trying desperately to get them to understand. "It was trying to get..."

"The pendant," Katerina answered softly, wrapping her fingers around his hand. "It was trying to get the pendant, but it's gone now. Everything is going to be okay."

He shook his head again, coughing even more. The floor around them was soaked with blood. Katerina and Cassiel watched the pool get bigger and bigger with worried eyes.

"Listen," he panted, "you have to listen to me..." Another round of coughing shook his body, leaving him pale and weak. "There was this creature—"

"We know," Cassiel said softly, taking his other hand. "Kailas killed it."

Dylan stared up at him in a daze, those blue eyes fluttering open and shut as he began to drift away. "...Kailas?"

Katerina nodded quickly, trying very hard not to cry. "That's right, honey. So try not to worry about it, okay? Everything's fine now. You're going to be fine."

Fine.

She didn't know why she kept saying the word. It couldn't be farther from the truth. Dylan was clearly not going to be fine. And she wasn't the only one to think so.

Cassiel had been staring at the ranger all the while, quiet indecision dancing in those dark eyes. But when the pool of blood reached the next floorboard, he seemed to make up his mind.

"Aidan—get over here!"

The vampire appeared a moment later, holding a sleeping Tanya under his arm.

"They were drugged," he panted, too caught up in what he'd seen in the next room to immediately grasp what was happening in this one. "It was a heavy sleeping draught, but I think—"

"Give him your blood," Cassiel commanded.

The vampire paused, staring at him in shock. A second later, his eyes drifted down to the ranger for the first time. The shock doubled. But this time it was paired with something else.

"I...I can't do that."

Katerina was staring between them, frozen perfectly still.

"You can, and you absolutely will." Cassiel got to his feet in a swift movement, grabbing Aidan by the back of the neck and pushing him down to his knees. "Give it to him—*now.*"

"No..." Dylan murmured weakly. "Cass, he can't—"

"Shut up," the fae snapped, his eyes never leaving the vampire. "Do it, Aidan. I won't tell you again. I'll just take it."

How he was planning on doing that, Katerina had no idea. But his best friend was bleeding out on a farmhouse floor, and the fae was no longer thinking straight.

Or maybe he is. Maybe that's the only way.

Aidan's handsome face was rigid and pale. He gave the fae a measured look before leaning deliberately away. "This is fear—not sense. It's permanent, what you're asking. It isn't the kind of connection you can break. It isn't the kind of life he wants to lead—"

"I couldn't give a *shit* about you vampires and your blood connections!" Cassiel's eyes flashed as he leaned forward, looking as dangerous as Katerina had ever seen. "If you don't do this now I will *kill* you, Aidan—I swear it!"

"Cass... stop," Dylan groaned, shivering as he coughed up even more blood. "He's right; I don't...I don't want it."

"I couldn't give a crap what you want," Cassiel replied, in an only slightly softer tone. "I'm not going to let you die here. I don't care what state that leaves you in. You'll be alive."

"Bound to me," Aidan stressed every word, those luminous eyes desperate for the fae to understand. "Closer than a friend, closer than a brother. It can even..." He trailed off, unwilling to finish. "Cass, there's a chance he may be all right—"

"THAT'S NOT YOUR CALL TO MAKE!"

"Stop it," Katerina whispered, bringing Dylan's hand up to her lips. His skin was cold, but she could still feel a pulse. It was faint, but it was there. "Stop it—both of you."

The fae made a sudden movement, like he was considering lunging at the vampire right then and there. Then Dylan let out a painful gasp that captured his complete attention.

"It was my fault," he said quietly, trying to push himself up. "It was a Shien. You can't let them get their hands on you." He tried again, oblivious to the fact that all three people were gently holding him down. "Where are Tanya and Sera? Are they all right?"

Katerina's heart was hammering in her chest, while the fae had gone very still. Both were focused less on what the ranger had said and more on the fact that he was speaking at all. There was a crispness to the words that hadn't been there before. His movements were weak but precise.

"They're fine," Cassiel said slowly, trailing a finger deliberately in front of the ranger's face.

Dylan followed every movement, looking frustrated he was being made to do so. Then, as if by carelessness, the fae dropped the prince's blade. The ranger caught it without batting an eye.

There was a breathless pause. Then Cassiel pushed gracefully to his feet.

"All right, then."

Dylan flashed a bloody grin, but Aidan and Katerina stayed right where they were. One frozen in shock. The other in equal parts shock and rage.

"All right?" Katerina repeated in a daze, staring up at him. "Just like that, you're going to—"

"If the Shien was searching for the pendant, then these creatures didn't descend upon this place at random. They were sent by the Red Knight." Cassiel swept quickly around the room, picking up whatever could be salvaged and slipping it into a bag. "We need to assume that more might be coming, and we certainly can't be here when they arrive. Dylan, can you stand?"

"Absolutely." The ranger pushed to his feet before collapsing in a pile of profanities and broken bones. "Just give me a second—"

"Aidan, can you carry him?"

The vampire didn't say a word. He just stood there, staring at the fae in silence.

...not good.

Katerina thought there was a decent chance she might run from the room if Aidan was looking at her like that. At any rate, she wouldn't keep packing—carelessly exposing her bare neck.

But the fae didn't look like he cared one way or another, and time was of the essence. The Shien hadn't exactly died peacefully, and the flames from its violent flailing were already starting to spread up the wall. Judging by the smoke drifting in from downstairs, the bacon had also caught fire in the kitchen. The farmhouse was made entirely of wood. There wasn't a moment to spare.

"Can you take him," Cassiel repeated with a touch of impatience, "or will the blood be too much? I know it's a temptation, but he doesn't have any to spare."

Katerina's mouth fell open in shock. One second he was demanding that Aidan rip open his veins, and now—

"I can take him."

Only decades of patience kept the vampire from attacking him right there. But he didn't have the luxury of giving in to those emotions. The house was coming down.

With an efficient sort of grace, he lifted Dylan into the air—blurring out of the room without saying another word. Katerina stared after him for a moment before glancing back at Cassiel. He was kneeling over the bed, murmuring something into Tanya's ear. The shape-shifter nodded, then wound her arms around his neck. She, too, was lifted. Kailas already had Serafina.

In a matter of seconds, the queen was alone in the room. She stared around in a kind of belated shock before catching sight of the golden pendant—still lying on the floor.

They'd almost forgotten it, she realized with a stab of surprise. All this fuss over the magical stone... and they'd almost left it in the farmhouse.

With the utmost care, she knelt down and recovered it from the ashes. It was stained with both soot and blood, but somehow it had never shone brighter. With a little sigh she slipped the chain over her head, feeling the familiar weight as it settled in the hollow of her neck.

"Katerina—get down here!"

She turned automatically to the door before glancing one last time at the room.

Just a few hours before Helen had been giving her the grand tour, pulling open the closet door and encouraging her to take any clothes she'd like. Tanya had been teasing her in the doorway, offering an extra blanket for the night. She'd kissed Dylan at the window before climbing up into bed. She'd been woken by the smell of bacon for breakfast.

...and then this.

Why can't things ever just be good? Why does everything always come crashing down?

Then a burning beam fell down from the rafters, and the voice called up to her again.

Without a backwards glance she hurried down the stairs, joining the others in the front yard. They'd taken what they could from the house, but the downstairs was already in flames. She stared at it for a moment, wondering if Richard and Helen were still inside, before following the rest of them around the side of the house to the barn.

The grass was strewn with the bodies of countless goblins, grotesquely disfigured and covered in blood, but the gang paid them no mind. Moving with the grim confidence of one who'd been doing it his entire life Cassiel freed the animals from their enclosure, then quickly bridled the horse. It was attached to the cart a second later, and the rest of them hurried to climb inside.

Katerina wished they could just slip away through the trees. She wished the day was over and that they'd never come to the farmhouse in the first place. If only wishing made it so.

The road that led to the village was long and flat. It gave a clear view of everything around it, so for the next ten minutes she sat in the back of the cart, perched on a bale of hay, watching the burning farmhouse getting smaller and smaller on the horizon.

A dozen miles away, she could still see the smoke.

Chapter 11

The cart was slow and the village was almost a full day away. Katerina doubted the gang said more than a total of ten words the entire time.

Serafina and Tanya were passed out in the hay, sleeping off whatever sedative had been released upstairs. They'd come to only briefly during the attack, and still had no real idea what had happened. The only reason Katerina wasn't drugged herself was that Dylan had left the window open after he'd carried her back upstairs to sleep.

That just left the men.

Kailas was at the front of the cart, eyes locked bleakly on the horizon as he silently guided the horses down the lane. Dylan had stayed awake long enough to demand Tanya's flask of whiskey before blacking out cold. And the vampire and the fae? The two weren't exactly speaking.

"You're on my cloak."

What? They weren't supposed to be speaking.

The two men were sitting across from each other near the tailgate of the cart. Arms resting on their knees. Staring vacantly at the rolling hills of grass. They had been that way for hours.

Cassiel startled at the interruption, lifting his eyes. "I'm sorry?"

Aidan's face was cold as he gestured sharply between them. "My cloak—you're sitting on it."

Cassiel's eyes lightened in surprise. He lifted his boots. "You're angry with me?"

Oh, seven hells...

Aidan froze dead still, and for a second Katerina thought he was going to strike the fae right then and there. She wouldn't blame him, but it was a fight she couldn't begin to imagine. The speed and precision of the vampire matched against the deadly grace of the fae.

Thankfully, he used his words instead. For now.

"Surely even you can't be that arrogant."

Cassiel stared back with honest surprise. "I don't—"

"Yes, I'm angry with you." Aidan's eyes flashed fiercely, a hint of temper breaking through that calm façade. "I'm angry that you demanded my blood, as if you had some holy claim to it. I'm angry that you threatened to butcher me in a farmhouse, just so your friend could suck on the bloody remains. I am *angry* with you, Cassiel."

The queen's eyes shot back and forth between them. She had recovered enough of a grip on her emotions to use her fire should it become absolutely necessary, but with Dylan's head resting in her lap she certainly hoped it wasn't going to come to that. At any rate, the entire gang was sitting on a bed of hay. But the fae didn't have any intention of fighting. He simply stared across the cart at the vampire, a peculiar emotion flickering in those clear immortal eyes.

"Aidan, I would do the same for you."

A strange hush fell over the cart. Kailas glanced over his shoulder, but kept his hands on the reins. Aidan was staring back in utter confusion, his forehead creased with a little frown.

"You..." He trailed off, shaking his head. "I don't know what that means."

"If the positions were reversed, if you were lying in Dylan's place. I would say whatever I had to, fight whoever I needed to, do anything that was necessary... if only to keep you alive."

It was suddenly quiet once again.

Katerina's eyes stung with secret tears and she lowered them swiftly to her lap. For his part, Aidan had no earthly idea what to say. He had frozen perfectly still, stunned into silence.

But the fae didn't require a response. To him, it was the simplest thing in the world.

"We're family now. We keep each other alive."

His lips curved with the hint of a smile.

"That's what families do."

THEY MADE IT TO THE village by nightfall. It seemed an unspoken assumption that each such provincial town was designed the same. It was easy to spot the bar and it was easy to spot the inn. In their first turn of good luck in hours, they were able to book rooms in one that catered to both.

By then the girls were awake. Tanya was begging for food, and Dylan was starting to get suspicious that someone had stabbed him in the chest.

"I'm telling you, it feels different," he insisted, fussing with his bandages as Katerina spooned him patient mouthfuls of stew. "I've been stabbed before, and this—"

"*Hey!*" She swatted his hand as he tried to peek underneath, burying it beneath the quilted bedspread for good measure. "What did we say about messing with the gauze?"

After a hushed deliberation, the friends had decided not to share every detail of what had happened—the stabbing being chief among of them.

The rationale was that Dylan was trying to heal and didn't need the added visual of one of his friends sliding a knife into his chest. The actual reason was that Cassiel, the friend in question, didn't want his unmedicated, homicidal friend knowing the fae had attacked him with a blade.

"I'm not messing with it, I just want to see—"

"Want to see what?"

The two looked up to see Cassiel standing in the doorway of their bedroom. There was a pair of sandwiches in his hand from the tavern downstairs, as well as two glass bottles.

"Dylan's trying to take off his bandages," Katerina answered with a strained look. "The man's convinced he's been stabbed."

Only someone watching very closely could have detected Cassiel's slight pause.

"Nonsense." He swept into the room like he owned it, perching gently on the foot of the bed. "Shien don't stab, they crush. Now stop messing with those bandages or I'll have to snap your ribs back into place. We all remember how fun it was the first time."

Dylan slumped back onto the pillows, trying very hard not to pout. "That's what Kat said..."

Cassiel relaxed a fraction of an inch. "Katerina's a smart woman." He gave her a smile that was half-grateful, half-threat. She'd better keep being smart, otherwise Dylan wouldn't be the only one to get a blade. Then the sandwiches dropped down between them, and he offered out a bottle to each. "I brought you ale."

Dylan grabbed his gratefully, snapping off the top. "This is why we're friends."

Cassiel's eyes flickered to his chest before flashing a sweet smile. "Yeah." Unwilling to press his luck the fae pushed swiftly to his feet, pausing only to stoke the fire as he swept gracefully towards the door. "Now get some rest and *don't* touch those bandages." He pointed a warning finger at the ranger's mummified torso. "I'll be back to check on them in the morning."

Dylan saluted sarcastically with the bottle. "Can't wait."

The door clicked shut behind him—so fast there wasn't time for anyone to see the queen's caustic glare. By the time Dylan glanced back at her, she was sipping ale with an innocent smile.

"How about it? You ready for some more stew?"

The urge to protest warred against the urge to smile. In the end he simply sighed, shifting himself higher on the pillows. "You don't have to feed me. I'm perfectly capable of—"

"Yes, yes. You're impossibly strong." She silenced him with a mouthful. "Probably made this stew yourself. Slaughtered the beasts with your bare hands."

"I'm pretty sure this is rabbit."

"Shush," she whispered soothingly. "Don't try to talk. You'll only strain yourself."

He chuckled painfully and bowed his head in defeat. There were some things on which his girlfriend was unwilling to compromise. His health was one of them. Stew was another.

"You know, I actually like you much better this way." She swept back his hair with a bright smile. "So broken and helpless. It's much more manageable."

It was a testament to just how broken and helpless that he didn't shove her off the bed. As it stood, it looked like he was seriously considering biting her hand.

"I'm glad you're enjoying yourself."

Her eyes danced with amusement as she set down the stew. "I'd be enjoying myself more in a bath."

His face went blank. Then he glanced at the adjoining door.

"Oh...you should." He leaned back against the pillows with a gallant smile. "Take your time, love. Try to relax. My only request is that you undress out here."

She rolled her eyes, sliding closer to him on the bed. "Actually... I was hoping you'd take one with me."

The smile faltered as he glanced again at the door. "Uh...I don't think so. Cass already—"

"Cassiel dumped a pitcher of water on you before wrapping a roll of bandages around your chest. That doesn't count, Dylan. You're still covered in blood."

"I can just use a wet towel—"

"A wet towel?" she repeated with an incredulous smile. "Why are you fighting this?"

He met her gaze for only a moment, then dropped his eyes to the bed. "It's a little difficult to move."

Difficult to move? His entire torso was being held together with stolen bandages and the miraculous healing power of a tavern sandwich.

She took his hand, giving it a sympathetic squeeze. "All the more reason for a relaxing soak. I can help you—"

"*No.*"

There was a pause. A muscle twitched in the back of his jaw.

"I can't—" He pulled in a sharp breath, eyes on the bed. "I can't walk, Katerina."

Katerina.

She couldn't remember the last time he'd used her full name.

It was always shouted in times of panic. When terrible creatures showed up at their door. It was never said in times like this. In a quiet room. When it was just the two of them.

She reached out slowly, lifting his face. "And how many times have you helped me walk?"

Time seemed to pause as she stared into those sky-blue eyes. Eyes that never ceased to sparkle, despite the sleeplessness-induced hollows bruised into his skin.

He pulled in a silent breath, then let it out in a sigh. "I'm a lot stronger than you."

"I'm sure I can manage—"

"I suffer from crippling male pride."

She bit down on her lip, trying hard not to smile. "Are we finished? Out of excuses?"

They stared off for a second more before he swung his legs over the side of the bed.

"Shouldn't have looked at you," he muttered under his breath. She shot him a questioning glance, and he rolled his eyes with a sigh. "That's what gets me into trouble. It's your damn eyes."

Oh really.

"Is that right?" she said airily, wrapping his arm around the back of her neck, ducking her head with a smile. "I never would have guessed."

There had been many times when Dylan had been injured before. Many times when he'd had to lean on her as they hobbled along some remote mountain trail. On every such occasion, it was manageable. On every such occasion, she was able to handle him with relative ease.

This was *not* one of those times.

"Kat, I can't—"

"It's all right," she soothed, feeling very much the opposite. "We're almost there."

His hand fisted in her hair as he struggled through one step after another. It was agony just to breathe, and with stolen sideways glances Katerina stared in horror at the lacework of bruises over his bare skin. They were black, the bruises. Not any other encouraging shade. Painted over his body in wide strips, suffered at the highest price. Made by only the vilest of creatures.

"Hang on." He released her and grabbed hold of the back of a chair, knuckles whitening as he held on with both hands. "Just give me a second."

That alone shocked her to the core. The ranger she knew had never asked for a second. Not even when a blood-thirsty dragon had swept down and plucked him into the sky.

"This was a bad idea," she whispered, staring at the tight bandages traversing his ribcage as her eyes started swimming with tears. "I'm sorry I suggested it. Let's just go back to—"

"No, we're almost there."

His face tensed as he tried to take a step before carefully lowering the same foot back to the floor. For a second he looked truly lost, staring down at a body that no longer answered to his command. Then he forced a neutral expression and flashed her a quick smile. "Go get it ready; I'll be there in a second."

It probably wasn't wise to leave him, but at this point she didn't protest. She simply patted him on the back, froze in horror at the extraordinary mistake, then vanished inside.

I PATTED him on the BACK?!

The slick tile sent a chill up her bare feet as she pumped the bellows and tipped the trough of heated water over the side of the tub. Spirals of steam rose from the surface as she did it again.

REALLY!?

"I only asked for one thing."

Katerina whipped around with a gasp.

Despite the waves of agony ripping through his body, a little grin played about Dylan's lips as he leaned against the doorjamb. A casual recline, but in this case he simply needed the support.

"Sorry?" A guilty blush heated the tops of her cheeks as she found herself drawn in by the magnetic power of those hypnotizing eyes. "What did you ask?"

He let her hang for a moment, biting his lip with a far more genuine smile.

"That you continue these preparations naked."

Her body hovered there for a second, like a puppet on a string, before all that aching tension vanished in a breathless sigh. She laughed lightly, tucking her hair behind her ears, before reaching up behind her and tugging at the crisscrossing ribbon that laced up the center of her back.

This was Dylan's favorite part—battling this ribbon. At first, it had baffled him. After a while, he could (and often did) untie it in his sleep. Now he could only watch.

"Slower," he instructed, taking great pleasure in her blushing cheeks. "Much slower. And if you wouldn't mind doing a little dance—"

She threw a shoe at him.

"Fine!" He threw up his hands with a painful laugh. "Fine. I'll dance."

A wave of laughter overtook her as she sashayed across the floor, coming up behind him with her arms wrapped around his waist. "I'd like to see you try."

He turned his head with a comeback, then froze. "What are you doing?"

This was her favorite part—though she had never been allowed to do it herself. She had always watched him from afar. Marveling in the lean perfection of his body. Heating with a silent thrill as his clothes fell to the floor, piece by piece. She'd always watched, never touched. While he might delight in dismembering her corsets, he had always undressed himself.

"Kat."

His body tensed and she felt him pull in a sharp breath. It was something she'd tried to do only once before, one of their first nights together at the castle. He'd stopped her then.

He was clearly about to stop her now.

"Sweetheart—"

"Let me," she whispered, reaching around to unclasp the buckle on his belt, sliding her fingers across the smooth skin on his waist. "Please."

The man had no problem being naked. In addition to being naturally brazen, like all shifters, he was completely unfazed by the concept of nudity. The undressing was the thing.

The thing he shied away from. The thing she craved.

He bowed his head and it took her a second to realize he was trembling. From the touch of her hands or from the pain, she couldn't tell. But when he caught her wrists, she wasn't surprised.

"Let's just get into the bath," he murmured.

She dropped her hands at once, pulling away from him with a wistful sigh as she slipped into the warm water. By the time she turned around, he'd removed the rest of his clothes. They were lying in a pile behind him as he nervously eyed the height of the tub.

"Having trouble?" she teased, sinking up to her chin with a devilish grin.

He flashed a look that made her very glad they were on the same side.

"I was just thinking of that demonic bounty-hunter that crushed me half to death. Kind of wishing it had crushed you instead..."

She snorted with laughter, rising quickly to take his arm. Together, with delicate motions, the two of them slowly climbed into the bath. With a shattered ribcage, it had been a mercy that he'd been unconscious when Aidan had laid him on the bed before. Things were looking the same now.

You got this, babe. Almost there.

He tried so hard to be silent, but a gasp of pain slithered between his teeth. *"Shit."*

"Are you okay?" she asked anxiously.

"Yeah, this is great." Every movement was stiff with pain as he sank into the water. "But, of course, you're known for your great ideas—" He broke off suddenly, his entire face transforming as his skin flushed with the steam. "Actually, I take it back. This is heaven."

And THAT'S why I suggested the bath.

His forehead fell against her hair as he let out a moan. A moan so theatrical and lustful and loud that she started giggling uncontrollably, nestling carefully into the circle of his arms.

"You've done it." He sank down with a smile, his battered body relaxing for the first time since they'd woken up in the castle. "You've cured me."

They lay there a few moments in silence.

"It was a demonic bounty-hunter?"

He let out a quiet sigh. "And we're back."

"I'm sorry." She twisted around to face him, keeping her weight carefully off his chest. "I just didn't grow up with the lore like you and others. I always feel like I'm a step behind..."

He caressed her sweetly, playing with a damp tendril of hair.

"I do know Shien are enforcers, mostly because not a creature alive can match them in strength. They aren't capable of much higher thought, so they tend to be used by more evolved creatures for dirty work in exchange for some kind of reward. At least, that's what Michael told me."

He stiffened upon hearing the name, then relaxed in the same instant. Like he was bracing for a blow that never seemed to fall. Katerina laced their fingers, staring at those faraway eyes.

"Are you angry with him? For never telling you?"

Dylan considered a moment, not entirely sure himself.

"It isn't Michael's way," he answered finally, "to be so direct. But in a sense, I think he tried to tell me. Tried to prepare me as best he could. No, I'm not angry with him."

They lapsed into silence again, lost in thought.

"Dylan," she whispered, almost afraid to say it out loud, "what if it isn't me?"

He startled slightly, like a man coming out of a dream. "What if *what* isn't you?"

"The prophecy." She shivered in the warm water, barely able to speak. "What if it's Kailas?"

His lips parted slightly, as if the possibility had never occurred to him. For a moment, he imagined a world in which it was true. A soft light shone in his eyes as they locked onto hers. "I would give *anything* for it to be Kailas."

She broke their gaze after only a moment. The light faded as quickly as it had come.

Of course he would.

Their hands stayed laced together, though neither continued to speak. He could tell the answer displeased her, but he meant it with all his heart. She would give anything to keep them together, but a secret part of her wished it was Kailas as well.

After what seemed like an eternity, Dylan closed his eyes with a sigh.

"*Run.*"

Her eyes snapped up, looking at him in surprise.

"What?"

The corner of his lips twitched up in a sad smile.

"Run," he said again, an echo of his desperate plea to her when he was bleeding out on the floor. "I want to tattoo it on your hand. So whenever you seem to forget, you can just look down."

The two fell into silence, both picturing the same scene. A shiver ran through the queen while the ranger stared down at the water, seeing monsters and dangers underneath.

"In what world would I run?" Katerina asked softly. He lifted his head and she met his gaze straight on. "In what world would I ever leave you?"

He brought her hand to his lips, pressing a soft kiss on her bruised knuckles. "...a world in which you stay alive?"

A strange feeling swept over her. A kind of bold certainty she was unable to ignore. Her eyes locked on his, and before she knew what was happening a quiet question passed between them. "You know I want to marry you, right?"

The room fell silent.

Dylan froze with his lips still grazing her knuckles, every muscle locking into place. She could almost see the frantic heartbeat, while on the outside he had never been so still.

A few seconds passed, then a few seconds more.

Then finally, he lifted his eyes. "I...I want to marry you, too."

It wasn't at all what she expected. He didn't look presumptuous or cocky, he didn't look triumphant or even particularly bold. He looked happy. And a little bit shy.

Then, all at once, his face paled in horror.

"I'm not asking," he blurted, his hands freezing over hers. "This is *not* me asking."

A wave of relief swept over her, shadowed by a wave of secret disappointment. She ignored them both—settling on amusement as she looked at the ranger's stricken face.

"Oh no?" she teased. "This wasn't your big moment?"

It took him a second to figure out she was joking, then he slowly let out a breath.

"I'm going to drown you in this bath."

There was a beat.

"So that's a no to the engagement?"

Another beat.

"Okay, then." He shifted forward, trying to lift his broken arms high enough to wrap them around her neck. "Drowning it is."

They struggled for a few seconds. Him trying his best to suffocate his girlfriend. Her trying her best to stop giggling as his efforts got more painfully pathetic with every pass.

"You're just going to have to slide under yourself," he said regretfully, gesturing to the water between them. "Don't try to hold your breath. Just give in. I'd do it myself, but—"

She silenced him with a kiss.

"...this doesn't spare you."

Another kiss. This time, he kissed her back.

They lay like that for a long time, wrapped in each other's arms, both thinking about all the close calls they'd had in the last twenty-four hours. Somehow, the relaxing bath made the list.

It wasn't until the water started getting cold that she twisted around, looking back at his face.

"Dylan, just based on our history..."

His arms stiffened as a look of caution flashed across his face. "Yeah?"

"The next time we're in alone in a quiet room..."

Even more caution. At this point, he was holding his breath. "Yeah?"

Their eyes locked.

"Don't ever tell me to *run*."

Chapter 12

The journey back to the bed was just as painful as the one to the bathtub. All those quiet, tender feelings vanished into a sea of threats and profanities as they hobbled slowly across the floor.

Of course, the second he touched the mattress Dylan blacked out immediately. Katerina glanced over, mid-sentence, to see him sprawled in the center of the bed. Lips slightly parted. Dark hair spilling gently across his eyes. She stared at him for a moment, almost dizzy with affection, then squeezed into whatever room was left, teetering precariously on the edge of the mattress.

The second she was lying down he rolled halfway on top of her. One arm slung across her waist, the other gripping the pillow. His face nestled in the hollow of her neck.

It was a much more vulnerable position than he usually slept. Almost clingy. He was still lying there when she opened her eyes the next morning.

"*Dylan*," she whispered, feeling the weight of his arm for the first time. It was borderline uncomfortable; on the other hand, it was the only thing keeping her from falling off the bed. "*Hon?*"

No response. The man was out cold.

Abandoning all dignity, she wriggled and squirmed until she escaped him. A second later, she fell with a thud onto the floor. He never opened his eyes.

Some ranger, she thought daintily, picking herself up and reaching for her clothes. *One near-death experience and he thinks it's permissible to sleep past noon.*

A sudden though made her pause.

Two near-death experiences.

Another pause.

Okay, three near-death—you know what? I'll let him sleep.

She dressed quickly and headed out into the open air. The sun was already high in the sky, and the village—which she hadn't gotten a good look at the night before—was in full swing.

Despite being so close to the castle, it was a town she had never seen. Probably because it was a little too poor, and a little too small. Back when they were kids, she and Kailas had been paraded around the local villages once a year. The *nicer* local villages. A 'royal tour.' It was meant to project some degree of relatability. Show the people that the monarchs were on their side.

As if the sight of a princess in a gilded carriage would somehow inspire the stable boy to think they would be given equal chances in life.

Of course, the tours only lasted for a couple of years. At that point, their father gave up on the idea of 'relatability' altogether and just started killing everyone.

"Good morning," she greeted a pair of young women as they passed her on the street, carrying bushels of clothing down to the river to wash. "Lovely day out."

They returned the greeting with automatic smiles, pausing only after they'd passed the queen to glance back at her on the street. There was something a little off about her. The precise clip of the vowels in a slightly more formal pattern of speech. Then there was that fiery hair...

They shared a questioning glance before continuing to the river with a shrug. Since the announcement of the accords, a number of strange and worldly people had filtered through the remote village. Enough to make the arrival of the blood-spattered caravan juicy gossip, but hardly enough to derail the entire day. The children still spun into a tizzy of course, but the adults had learned to hide their curiosity carefully. To wonder only in silence, to be revisited on a later date.

Katerina felt their eyes and paused, then relaxed when they went on their way. She wondered if they'd heard about the fire. She wondered if they'd known Richard and Helen. Then she tried very hard to put away all thoughts of Richard and Helen. Fortunately, she was about to have help.

There was a sudden commotion and she turned to see a truly bizarre sight.

Cassiel was sitting at an outdoor table surrounded by a cluster of children. Their heads were bent together, and he seemed to be telling them some kind of story. They stood on their tiptoes as his eyes got very serious, then jumped back with peals of laughter when he threw up his hands. More and more flocked around him. One brave little girl had even dared to sit on his lap.

The queen froze where she stood, staring in fascination.

Her first impulse was that it must be vanity; however, Cassiel had never needed an audience for that sort of thing, and there was a genuine affection in those sparkling eyes. As for the children, they clearly adored him. The girl was playing with the fringe on his cloak. The others were staring in fascination at his long ivory hair. Then one made the supreme mistake of asking to see his ears.

...not good.

The Fae weren't known for their even tempers, and their prince was a prime example. She had once seen him lash a man with a cattle prod for asking if it was true that the Fae didn't sleep.

This toddler didn't stand a chance.

Much to her surprise he indulged them, sweeping back his hair with a little smile. A chorus of delighted squeals echoed up and down the street. Of course, when they asked to touch them he assured them that hell was much worse for little children and they ran away in tears.

Katerina pursed her lips and made her way over, sinking into the chair by his side. "Making friends?"

He nodded absentmindedly, taking a long drink of something that smelled of cinnamon and cloves, before abruptly setting down the glass. "You and Dylan didn't have sex, did you?" He returned her scandalized expression with a reproachful glare. "Those walls are like paper, Katerina."

She froze in sheer mortification, then remembered Dylan's theatrical moan.

"No!" she exclaimed quickly. "Not at all, we were just... wait—why am I explaining this to you?! I get that you guys are friends, Cass, but it's *really* none of your business!"

"He is in no condition to indulge you, princess." The fae lifted a chiding finger. "That beast virtually cracked him in half. You must control yourself—heaven knows he has no control himself."

Unable to decide whether to slap him, laugh, or pull out her own hair, Katerina simply shut her eyes. Breathing in through the nose, out through the mouth. The way she'd done as a child. "Thank you, Cassiel. I'll certainly keep that in mind."

He nodded curtly, utterly immune to sarcasm, and together the two of them turned back to the street. Like most impoverished places Katerina had seen, the tiny village seemed improbably happy. Yes, the people worked hard, but they'd developed a strong sense of community. The kind of bonds you'd wouldn't find in a castle or aristocratic court. They approached each task with good humor and a fierce kind of pride, and everything they drank seemed to smell exactly like a holiday.

Cassiel said it was called chai. He quickly ordered her a glass.

The children were by far the highlight.

Roving the street in little packs. Armed with an impressive array of sticks. Colliding every now and then in the middle, where they proceeded to wage war.

Cassiel watched them playing with a little smile. He even returned their ball when it rolled to a stop at their feet. For her part, Katerina kept her eyes on the fae. Ceaselessly surprised. Reveling in a part of his personality she'd never seen, one she would never have expected.

"You ever think about having kids?" she asked curiously.

"Of course," he answered without hesitation. "I love children. I would love to have children of my own."

It surprised her, then it didn't. She remembered what Tanya had said about the Fae having large families (when they managed to have families at all). Then she remembered what Cassiel had said about his council being obsessed with the idea of repopulation.

They wanted their prince to have children. They wanted those children to be Fae.

"When I was growing up, there were great story halls in Taviel," he said unexpectedly. "The elders would gather the children in a circle and we'd listen as they told us tale after tale. Adventures of knights and kings. Fearsome warriors and starlit maidens. We sat there for hours," he reminisced, a faint glow of nostalgia warming his eyes. "It's how we learned our history. The great fables of old."

He felt her staring and shook it off briskly.

"No one to tell them to now."

With a rush of sadness, Katerina realized that as a child he must have had every intention of becoming one of those elders when he grew up. Of passing on the stories himself. Watching his own children gather in the great hall and play in the ivory citadel.

"It must be lonely," she murmured.

He cocked his head quizzically, and she looked down with a flush.

"I just mean... all these years. Endless years. But all those people are gone."

Those dark eyes settled on her face, and for a moment she found herself regretting having gotten out of bed. Then, to her extreme astonishment, he threw back his head with a laugh.

"My dear princess, you have just discovered the eternal conundrum of immortality." He shook his head, still chuckling. "This chai is really working for you."

She relaxed into her chair with a nervous smile, discreetly scanning for a cattle prod. But at the same time she kept her eyes on his beautiful face, waiting for an answer to her question.

He quieted after a moment, staring off into space.

"It's lonely."

Such a simple answer to encapsulate a grief that had lasted hundreds of years. But what else was there to say? And who was left to listen?

"So how does Tanya fit in with all that?"

A highly personal question, but the man had just instructed her not to have sex. Highly personal revelations seemed the kind of thing that people shared over chai.

And she so desperately wanted to know.

If he ever imagined himself as a father, was Tanya in that picture, too? Were the children ivory-haired warriors, or mohawked little misfits with toddler-sized flasks of ale?

"Tanya?"

The same image must have occurred to him as well, because he threw back his head with another sparkling laugh. The kind only the shape-shifter was able to solicit. Completely unrestrained.

"After five hundred years, everything starts to feel the same. Tanya's different."

The two shared a fleeting smile before turning back to the street.

Another simple answer to an infinitely complicated question. A part of her wanted to ask more, but she let it go. He didn't know what the future held any better than she knew it herself. For now, they were simply content to sit there together. People-watching in silence. Drinking their chai.

"My lord?"

The two friends lifted their heads as a boy of about eight or nine pulled himself away from the rest of the group, tentatively venturing closer to the table. Cassiel offered him a gracious smile.

"Yes, child, what is it?"

The boy cocked his head, staring in wonder at the High-Born prince. Completely oblivious that his own sovereign, the Queen of the High Kingdom, was sitting by his side.

"That blade you were telling us about—what was it called?"

"It's a scimitar," Cassiel answered patiently. "It's used for decapitation."

The boy nodded fervently. "And what's decap—"

"*Okay*," Katerina interrupted quickly, "run along now."

The child vanished into the crowd as she turned with exasperation to the fae. He was predictably unconcerned. He did, however, seem to find her anonymity quite amusing.

"Perhaps you should start wearing your crown out amongst the people," he suggested lightly. "Then there might be a chance some of them would know who you are."

She opened her mouth with a withering reply, then slumped back in defeat. "I was thinking the same thing."

The rest of the hour passed quickly. Despite their playful bickering the two hadn't gotten a chance to simply talk together in months, and each had missed the other more than they were willing to say. The table in front of them was littered with empty glasses and they were just about to order another round, when a sudden shout echoed from the tavern.

Guess who's awake...

Katerina didn't need the fae's heightened senses to hear the tortured cry. And she didn't need to speak whatever language Dylan was cursing in to understand the gist.

"Completely uncivilized." The fae set down his drink with a sigh, pushing to his feet. "I understand the man's part wolf, but he's basically feral."

"You're the ones who vowed to spend your lives together," Katerina answered sarcastically, following him back across the street. "I'm just the girl he decided to love."

BY THE TIME THEY GOT back to the tavern, the others had heard the noise and assembled in the room. Tanya was perched in the windowsill, carving her name with a rusted blade. Serafina and Kailas were balanced on the edge of the bathtub, determined to make no mention of the blood. Aidan was pacing in front of the dresser, while Dylan was waiting in the center of the room.

"Good *morning*," he said the second they stepped inside.

There was something strange about the way he stressed the word and the pair instinctively paused, warily staring back at him. It took a second for Katerina to realize what was different. For her to see the stray bits of thread on the edge of his bandage.

"So guess what?" Dylan continued with that same murderous look. "I woke up alone this morning, *unsupervised*, and discovered the most shocking—"

"Dylan, I hope you didn't remove your bandages," Cassiel interrupted seriously. "Because I happen to know that would make Katerina unbelievably angry."

The room fell silent. Then the fae gave her a discreet nudge.

"Angry *and* disappointed," she added quickly. "You promised that you weren't going to touch it last night. I hope I can count on your word."

There was a heavy pause. A pause during which the ranger looked like he might actually explode. Then he bit down on his lip, forcing a rigid smile. "Of course you can."

"At any rate," Cassiel continued cheerfully, "I'm sure everything that happened was in your very best interest. Aside from the Shien almost crushing you to death."

"Really?" Dylan's voice was dangerously sweet. "Because it feel like someone stabbed me between the ribs." His eyes flashed as he touched a specific spot. "Right here."

Yep—that's the spot.

The fae stepped closer, staring him right in the eyes. "But you can't know for sure, can you?"

A low growl rumbled deep in the shifter's chest, and for a moment he looked just as feral as Cassiel had said. Then his eyes flickered guiltily to Katerina before dropping to the floor. "No, I can't."

There was a cool rush of air as the men stepped away from each other. One with a secret silently dancing in his eyes. The other looking like he wanted to burn the building to the ground.

Instead, he turned to Aidan. "I wanted to apologize for what Cassiel said back on the farm," he said abruptly, catching the vampire by surprise. "His parents died before they could teach him any manners."

Cassiel settled down on the bed with a grin, while Aidan glanced between them—looking very much like he wanted to be left alone. "That isn't really—"

"Do vampires have parents?" Tanya asked suddenly, still playing with the rusted knife.

Aidan flashed her a quick glance before returning to his pacing. "You know those deep shadows you can only see when there's fog?"

"Yeah," she said excitedly.

"Well, every full moon, we just spring up out of those."

Kailas and Serafina laughed quietly, while the smile faded from the shifter's face. Her eyes narrowed as she stared across the room, beginning to suspect he wasn't telling the truth.

"We need to figure out what to do," Aidan said suddenly, before she could speak again. The others turned to him at the same time. "First at the castle, then at the farm...we don't know if those evils were chasing us, or if it's merely the Knight's darkness spilling into the land. But either way, we don't have any time to waste. The Hempers were the first casualties. There will be many more."

The *Hempers*. Katerina had already begun to forget their last name.

"Kerien was the first casualty," Cassiel said softly. "But Aidan's right. We need to go."

"Go where?" Kailas asked, one hand absentmindedly rubbing his shoulder. The others had taken the last few nights to heal as best they could but, like Katerina, he was recovering at a slow, human pace. "The man's been missing for hundreds of years. We have no idea where he is now."

"One problem at a time," Dylan murmured, sitting slowly on the desk. "We might not know where he is, but the crown is in Taviel. And he'll be looking for it. That's still our best bet."

"And how far away is that?" Katerina asked. She had avoided the question thus far, more out of pessimism than anything else, but it was time to make a concrete plan.

Instead of answering, Dylan gestured to the Fae. They shared a quick glance before Serafina clammed up and Cassiel bowed his head with a weary sigh.

"It's far, but not impossible." His eyes flashed up to Dylan. "We're going to need a ship."

A ship?!

"Are you sure?" Even the ranger was unable to hide his surprise. "That's a different kind of... we won't be in control on a ship."

"It's the fastest way," Cassiel replied quietly. A strange look came over him, a memory still fresh enough to cause pain. "When Sera and I left, it was on a ship."

It was silent for a moment before Aidan ventured, "Why can't Katerina just fly?"

She'd been thinking the same thing herself. Even though her power was a bit temperamental at the moment, that had only ever impeded the fire—never her ability to shift.

"I could help," Kailas volunteered quietly. "If it was too far... we could split the difference."

Both Katerina and Dylan glanced at him at the same time, both of them thinking the same thing, but the fae merely shook his head. "A dragon could never make it across the sea. There isn't anywhere for it to touch down. It's one of the reasons Taviel was so remote—for protection."

"And once we cross the sea?" Katerina asked.

Cassiel spoke slowly, weighing every word. "We could try." He shared a quick look with Dylan. "It might help...but it might also draw the Red Knight's army right to our door."

"You do look kind of like a target up there," Tanya agreed reluctantly. "It really doesn't help that you're bright red. Maybe we could paint you—"

"Not on your life."

"So it's settled," Aidan brought them back on point. The queen's blood had faded from his system and it looked like he was back in control. "We'll buy passage on a ship."

"Why can't we just buy a ship?" Tanya argued.

Cassiel's face lightened with the hint of a smile. "Someone's gotten spoiled living in a castle." She shrugged unapologetically. "We don't have that kind of money with us. And even if we did—I don't know how to sail a ship."

Her mouth fell open in shock. "You don't?"

It was quite possibly the first time the fae had admitted any deficiency in his life. His smile sharpened as he cocked his head with a little spite. "Do you?"

"No," she answered slowly, "but I haven't been alive for hundreds of years."

"I also can't bake bread. Those are the only two things."

"You are so distractible—all of you!" Aidan shouted.

The room fell suddenly quiet. The others had never heard him shout before. He was always so carefully contained, the vampire. Never the one to lose control.

He saw them staring and bowed his head with a sigh, running a hand back through his dark hair. "I'm sorry. I need to feed."

If possible, this was even more shocking. Not the fact that he needed more blood so quickly, but that he was willing to say it out loud. Like most vampires, Aidan had always been very cagey when it came time to feed. He never talked about it. Most of the time, he preferred to do it alone.

"Already?" Dylan's voice sharpened slightly as he and the vampire locked eyes. "I happen to know that you had rather a lot. And quite recently."

...just kill me now.

"That was to heal." Aidan sounded almost apologetic, looking like he wished he hadn't said anything at all. "I used it to replenish, not to feed."

The room fell silent once more, everyone avoiding everyone else's gaze.

"Then let's make haste." Serafina pushed to her feet. "This town was built on the banks of a river. They won't have the type of ship we're looking for, but they should have something that can get us to the sea. If we trade some of the things we brought with us, we might be able to afford it."

And what about when we get to the sea?

No one wanted to answer that question. One problem at a time.

THE THINGS THE GROUP had brought with them turned out to be mainly jewelry. None of the friends had had time to grab anything from the castle before they left, which left whatever the women happened to be wearing, along with whatever of Petra's supplies had escaped the fire.

"I'll get you another one," Kailas said softly, kissing the side of Serafina's neck. "I promise."

The white diamond bracelet she'd tried to give Helen as payment passed into the hands of a greedy merchant—a man who couldn't believe his luck. Already he was muttering excitedly about how best to dismantle it, what price he could fetch for the individual stones.

"You don't think I have enough diamonds?" she asked lightly.

But there was a wistfulness in the way she stared after it. So exquisite in the stranger's dirty hands. Katerina wondered again under what circumstances Kailas had given it away.

"There's no blood."

The queen startled slightly as Aidan came up to stand beside her, his dark eyes catching the light of the setting sun. His hands were in his pockets, seemingly relaxed, but there was a rigidness to the way he was standing. An underlying agitation he couldn't seem to control.

"In the whole village?" she asked in surprise. "The butcher—"

"Just dumped out the entire supply," Aidan finished briskly. The corner of his lips twitched as he watched the merchant's exchange. "And I don't think he had any idea why I was asking."

Katerina laughed softly, bowing her head.

When they were living back at the castle, it had seemed like ages since the friends had been on the road. The wilderness adventure, as perilous as it was, seemed like another lifetime. Something out of a dream. Katerina would lie awake for hours each night, trying to preserve it in her memory.

Now here they were again.

"I wouldn't be so worried about it," the vampire continued quietly, "except for the ship..."

Katerina's eyes widened as she suddenly understood.

Trapped on a ship with a limited manifest, with limited crew, and no idea how long they were going to be out on the open water? It was every vampire's worst nightmare.

"There has to be something in the next port," she said confidently. "Wherever the river meets the sea, wherever we stop to find a ship...they're bound to have something."

Or someone.

Aidan nodded silently, bowing his head, while the young queen stared at him with growing concern. Already she could see the bluish outline of veins spidering up his pale skin, the bruise-like hollows beneath his eyes. Truth be told, she didn't know if he was going to make it to the next port.

And she had no idea what would happen if he went too long without blood.

"So I found us a boat."

The pair turned around as Dylan strode up behind them, his weathered cloak whispering across the ground. The sight of it brought a secret smile to Katerina's face—no matter how dire the circumstances. It looked so much more natural on him than a crown.

"There's a local fisherman who heads down to the sea port twice a month. He was going to go next week, but for half of what we have left he said we can leave at first light."

Half of what we have left—that isn't going to leave anything for the actual ship.

"Is that...is that something we can afford?" Katerina asked quietly.

"No," the ranger admitted, "but I don't see any alternative. We'll just have to..." He trailed off in confusion, staring at something just over her head.

"...so pretty..."

Katerina spun around, staring at the merchant who was still standing with them.

"...pretty enough to eat..."

In a flash, the merchant crammed Serafina's diamond bracelet right into his mouth—crunching down on the stones before forcing himself to swallow. A few drops of blood trickled from the corner of his mouth as he let out a laugh. The friends stared at him in astonishment, too surprised to move.

"Are you all right?" the fae asked in concern, laying a soft hand upon his arm. "Why...why on earth would you do that?"

He stared at her face, stared at her hand, then let out another bloody laugh. "Oh yes, miss. Quite all right."

The friends were still staring when Cassiel and Tanya joined them. Their castle clothes had been cleaned and sold to the highest bidder, and they were dressed for a journey as well.

"All right, we've packed up everything from the tavern—"

"We're staying another night in the tavern," Dylan interrupted. "I found us a boat, but it doesn't leave until morning."

Tanya cast an irritated glance over his shoulder, eyeing the fisherman she believed to be responsible. "Well, offer to pay him more money so we can leave tonight." In a building over her shoulder, a woman jumped from the second story. "It's a difference of twelve hours, Dylan."

Wait, jumped from the—

"My lord?"

Cassiel looked down in surprise to see a little girl tugging on the corner of his cloak. It was the same one who'd climbed into his lap when he was telling the children stories. Maybe two or three years old. Blue eyes, curly brown hair, and dimples tucked into both cheeks.

He knelt down immediately, softening in surprise when she took him by the hand.

"What is it, little one?"

Her eyes widened as she bounced up on her toes, cupping a hand around her mouth as if to tell him a secret. Utterly perplexed he leaned down farther, placing a gentle hand on her back as she stretched up to whisper into his ear...

...and sank her teeth into his face.

What the—!

For a second, the handsome fae simply froze. Then he jerked away with a gasp. At least, he tried to. The girl was latched onto his cheekbone, those tiny teeth embedded deep in his skin.

"Cass!"

Dylan's hand flew to his sword, then stopped cold.

What was he going to do? Kill a child?

With blind instinct the fae caught the girl by the face, prying her away with remarkably gentle hands. At first, she resisted. Then she suddenly let go, staring up at him with a giant, gap-toothed smile, trickles of blood dripping down her little chin.

"...so pretty..."

The friends froze at the same time, then turned around slowly. The merchant was standing right behind them, staring at Serafina with a dreamy smile.

"...pretty enough to eat..."

Oh, crap.

He lunged before any of them were ready, knocking the graceful woodland princess right off her feet. She landed on the ground with a gasp of surprise, surprise that turned to a scream of terror the second the man sank his teeth into her skin.

This time, Dylan had no problem using his sword.

But Kailas was already using his fire.

The merchant dissolved in a pile of ashes, leaving the breathless princess in his wake. She stared down at the gash in her leg as both men lifted her to her feet. Shock white and trembling.

"...what's happening?"

The little girl was laughing. A sound so light and bubbling it had no business coming out of that bloody face. Cassiel took a step back, staring at her in horror.

"Dylan, we should leave *right* now."

The ranger paled, lifting his eyes behind them. "I don't think it's that simple."

With a feeling of dread, the others followed his gaze. Staring up at the little village that had welcomed them with open arms. Only to see every single villager staring right back.

Crap. We're already too late.

Chapter 13

It was a nightmare come to life. The one where you were frozen and everyone was staring in shock.

Only this time, all those people had decided to eat you as well.

The friends slowly backed down the bank of the river, not stopping until their boots actually touched the frothy waves. It wasn't deep. They could surely swim across. But wouldn't that mean that all the villagers could do the same? On the opposite bank, there was very little cover.

But these people aren't evil! They're not demons or monsters! They're just people!

The little girl was still laughing, Cassiel's blood streaming down her face. He lifted a hand to his cheek, looking like he was going to be sick. "I take it back; I don't want to have kids."

The others kept backing away, but in spite of himself the fae froze where he stood. Eyes locked on the barefoot child. Looking like his heart was about to break.

"We can't leave them," he said, his voice almost breaking.

Tanya's face was pale but decided. "Yes, we absolutely can."

They spoke in a whispered hush, afraid to make their voices any louder. Already, the people standing closest to them had started closing in. But still the fae didn't move.

"They're innocent." Cassiel couldn't tear his eyes away from the child. "They don't want to be doing this—"

"What they want is to *eat* us," his girlfriend snapped. "Ask your sister. Ask your face."

"They haven't turned on each other," Dylan said quietly. "Only us." His eyes flickered between the child and the fae, softening ever so slightly. "She's not in danger, Cass."

Kailas turned pale, glancing at the pile of ashes that used to be the merchant. Katerina edged away from the fisherman, reaching without thinking to take Aidan's hand.

"Should I shift *now*?" Kat looked around slowly, taking in where it would be safest.

The vampire shook his head, staring at the people closing in. "You shift now and the Knight will know exactly where to find us."

"But he clearly already knows where we are," Serafina argued.

And how does THAT keep happening?!

The villagers were getting closer every second.

"Either way, we can't just stand here." Katerina shifted her weight nervously, backing farther into the river. "We need to come up with a—"

She broke off with a shrill scream, falling face-first into the water.

A sharp pain laced up her side as she thrashed and flailed in the water. Something was grinding into her ribcage. The dusky blue had begun to cloud with swirls of red. She opened her mouth with a silent scream. Two hands were holding her down, and then—

Her head broke through the surface with a wild gasp.

Every one of her friends had leapt into the water after her, but it was Tanya who'd pulled her free. One hand was gripped around Katerina's cloak as the other wedged against the thick neck of the man who'd grabbed her. The same man she'd seen selling loaves of bread only hours before.

"A little help?" she asked through gritted teeth.

Dylan dispatched him with a single blow, then grabbed his falling body and dragged him reluctantly to the shore. He was already stirring by the time his head hit the sand. But that was the very least of their problems. Katerina's scream had broken the stillness.

The villagers had started to run.

THE PLAN WAS TO STAY together. It didn't need to be said. The plan was always to stay together.

But somehow that never worked out.

Capable as they were, united as they were, the gang fell back under the sheer number of the people crashing into them. People who didn't seem to care for their own safety. People whose only concern was the seven teenagers standing in front of them. Teenagers who scattered like the wind.

Tanya and Serafina disappeared into the tavern where they'd been staying. Cassiel and Kailas vanished the opposite way. Dylan and Aidan got pushed farther back into the water. And Katerina?

For one of the first times, the young queen was completely on her own.

She heard them shouting for her, heard sounds of a distant fight, but was unable to see anything through the swarm of bodies that had pushed in between. A fierce blow landed on the back of her head. A woman's hand tangled roughly in her hair. She threw her arms in front of her face, trying instinctively to protect it, only to have the owner of the tavern bite down on her wrist.

"Help!" she screamed, twisting wildly to get away. "Someone help!"

In an act of desperation she actually ducked into the river, squinting as best she could against the murky water as she weaved between the legs of the townspeople. Whatever affliction had seized them, it didn't leave much room for higher thought. The second she vanished from sight, they were utterly at a loss as to what to do.

Unfortunately, that meant the whole lot of them turned to Dylan and Aidan.

The second Katerina's eyes peeked above the churning waves it was clear that the men were having a hard time. Both of them were gifted with enough deadly talents to lay the whole village to the ground, but neither one was willing to risk serious harm to even a single inhabitant.

Broken, bruised, and battered, they still had more ability and strength than the villagers.

They tempered the violence instead. Checking their strength. Pulling their punches. Aidan had yet to even lower his fangs. But the people coming after them were trying to kill, and that sort of restraint was already landing them in a world of trouble.

"Kat!"

Dylan saw her the moment she broke through the surface. His face cleared with unspeakable relief, but before he could start to make his way over the village blacksmith stepped into his path.

Either by intention or unlucky coincidence, the man punched him right in the ribs.

NO!

The ranger doubled over with a tortured scream, reaching instinctively to the vampire for balance. Like they were connected by a string Aidan whirled around and caught him right before he could disappear beneath the choppy water, pulling him along as they backed farther into the river.

The fight was over. They were in full retreat.

And there was absolutely no way to reach them.

Breathe. Remember to breathe.

The villagers hadn't seen her yet. That was her only advantage.

As quietly as she could, she eased back into the water and did the unthinkable. She moved away from her friends and headed out on her own. They had made it to the far shore, much faster than the people pursuing them. Dylan was half-dazed by pain, but with the vampire's speed they would still be able to mount some kind of defense. It was ugly, but they'd been through worse.

So stop worrying about them and start worrying about yourself!

There were two options, two sides of the shore. But one of them was sparse and swarmed with possessed townsfolk and the other had plenty of places of hide.

I'll just make my way across. She broke it down into pieces, trying to remain calm. *I'll make my way across and try to get to the tavern. I could have sworn I saw Sera and Tanya go inside—*

Then a little girl standing at the edge of the mob slowly turned around. There was blood on her face, brackish moss in her hair. Her fingers were curled into tiny claws.

Their eyes met for a split second and a single thought flashed through the queen's mind.

Get out of the water!

Without bothering to keep quiet, she spun around and started kicking frantically towards the shore. A few other people turned, drawn by the noise, but by the time they caught sight of her she was already racing up the sandy path—her wet cloak trailing behind her, red hair flying in the wind.

She slid to a stop at the entrance to the courtyard, staring around up and down the street.

Her first thought was that the village was by no means as deserted as it had looked from the river. Her next thought was that there were still plenty of places to hide.

A pack of stable boys lurched past her as she crouched low to the ground, darting from store front to store front, trying not to be seen. It was slow work. And there was a huge stretch of open ground she'd have to cross in order to get to the tavern. The only good news was that Dylan was right. The villagers didn't appear to be hurting one another.

This is because of us, she thought miserably. *This is because we broke the curse and set the man free.*

Faster and faster she ran, cursing her long dress as it whipped around her ankles. With her luck, she was going to trip and knock herself out before making it to the tavern. She'd wake up to the locals feasting on her clumsy body and her final thought would be *I should have been wearing pants.*

There was a sudden noise behind her and she stifled a shriek.

In a flash she crouched behind a water barrel, watching as the town butcher stalked out of his cottage, dragging a blood-soaked knife.

Animal or person? Animal or person?

Katerina stared with wide eyes at the blade, wondering if any of her friends was responsible for the little ribbon of crimson that trailed behind it into the dirt. She couldn't imagine this stocky, aging man getting the better of anyone she knew, but they weren't exactly playing by the rules. Not only were those same friends trying to protect the people attacking them, but the people attacking them weren't in the most predictable state of mind.

Case in point.

With absolutely no warning, the man threw down the knife and started crawling on his hands and knees through the village square. None of the other people milling around seemed to think this was at all unusual, and a second later he got back to his feet. Only this time, his face was smeared with dirt and there was a hungry look in his eye.

Get to the tavern.

The queen was shaking with debilitating waves of fear. No matter what she did, she was unable to catch her breath. Everything the seven of them had been through and *this* was the time she got separated? Trapped in a village of cannibals, with nowhere to run and no end in sight?

She'd rather be back in Carpathia, squaring off against a dozen lions. At least then there'd be no blurring of lines. At least then she could use her fire to fight—

"What do we have here?"

A quiet voice made her jump in fright, and she whirled around to see the pair of women she'd greeted earlier that morning. The ones who'd been carrying laundry down to the river.

They were studying her carefully. She was shocked they were able to speak.

"Can you...can you understand me?"

They paused for a moment, then the woman standing closer inclined her head.

"Oh, thank heavens!" Katerina pulled them down behind the barrel with her, whispering frantically. "Listen, something's happened and we need to get out of here. Do either of you have any idea where we can—"

"This is a pretty dress."

The queen stopped mid-sentence, staring down at the woman's hand. It was wrapped around the folds of her skirt, tendons straining beneath her pale skin.

A little shiver laced up Katerina's arms and she slowly leaned away. "Th-Thank you."

Run!

But she was afraid to move. Afraid it would set them off.

"I want it," the other girl blurted. Then her head jerked to the side and she corrected herself. "I mean, I want one like it. For me."

Katerina nodded quickly, still backing away. Her eyes glistened with tears.

"Give it—" the second woman cut off with a sigh of frustration that suddenly escalated into a full-on shout. "Give it to me!"

By now, the commotion had caught the attention of the other villagers. They had frozen where they stood, staring with vacant expressions at the trio of girls.

"You...you can have it." Katerina was on her feet by now, backing away more quickly. It would just be a short run to the tavern, but there were several people standing in between. The women straightened up with her and she tried to stall. "Just give me a second to—"

With a feral cry, the woman lunged.

NOOO!

Katerina leapt back just as the woman's nails scraped down the side of her face, causing her to scream without thinking. The sound only excited the rest of them, and before she could blink the blood from her eyes they had snapped out of their collective trance and were in full pursuit.

"Katerina!"

She could have sworn she heard someone call her name, but there was no time to turn and see who it was. People were closing in from every side, getting closer and closer. She sucked in gasping breaths of air. Her feet pounded the packed dirt as she sprinted beneath the eaves.

Then a fist caught her in the stomach and she went sprawling into the road.

A tall man was standing over her, squinting slightly as if he had never seen something quite like her before. One hand was still curled into the fist that had struck her, and the other reached up slowly to scratch the sides of his beard. A trail of blood followed his fingernails.

For a split second, they simply froze. Then everything seemed to happen at once.

Katerina scrambled backwards just as the man leapt forward, catching her by the ankles and slamming her back into the ground. The force of it knocked the wind out of her. Before she knew what was happening he was crawling on top of her, crushing her beneath his weight.

"No! Please stop! No!"

A part of her knew it wouldn't do any good, but she couldn't help but scream. The man's mouth opened automatically and he leaned down, eyeing the skin beneath her collarbone.

Her eyes glazed over in terror. Her arms buckled and bent. But all at once, just seconds before he could touch her, the strangest thing happened.

She heard Dylan's voice inside her head.

What are you going to do now, princess?

Her body startled in surprise, then went instinctively still. It was a question she'd heard a hundred times before. Pinned down in a hundred different positions during their training.

If she closed her eyes, she could almost see it.

The brutish villager vanished, and instead the handsome ranger was lying on top of her. A little smile playing around his lips. A little twinkle in his eye as he repeated the question.

Now you've got me here, princess. What are you going to do?

A sudden rush of feeling swept back into her deadened limbs as she remembered something very important: She was not helpless. She had learned to fight back.

Where's my weight?

The man was crushing the top half of her, but that left her legs relatively free. With just a bit of squirming, she was able to twist to a different angle and knee him right in the stomach.

It worked! She couldn't believe it worked!

The man instantly released her, rearing back in surprise. She didn't have to think before landing another two kicks right in his chest, toppling him backwards into the road.

That's good, princess. Now always remember to watch your—

A strike to the temple left her momentarily senseless, and she fell to her knees as the sky exploded in stars. She blinked rapidly, raising a dazed hand. But before she could begin to recover two hands grabbed her by the back of the cloak, lifting her roughly to her feet.

The town midwife didn't want to eat on the ground. She preferred to do it standing.

Katerina's wits returned just as the woman came at her, a set of dulled teeth aiming for the queen's slender neck. She had just enough time to duck then reacted without thinking, spinning out to the side before flipping the woman cleverly onto her back.

Aidan had taught her that move. Interestingly enough, most of the tactics he'd shown her involved one person evading another person who was trying to bite their neck.

Go figure, little leech.

That voice was back, guiding her along with sarcastic commentary as, one by one, she took down the people standing in her path.

Left hook to the face. What are you doing to do?

The queen staggered back, dazed and reeling.

Well I'd duck a little faster than that, but it was the right idea. On your right—

This time she dropped almost completely to the ground, sweeping the minister's legs out from under him before cracking his head against a slab of stone.

At this point, I'd probably make a pun.

On and on she went, picking up more confidence with every turn. In a strange way, it was the perfect opportunity for her to test out her skills. The dragon was the trump card, and she wasn't allowed to use it. The fire would be lethal, and she didn't want to kill. But, unlike the soldiers and monsters and demonic nightmares that had made recent cameos in their lives, these were people.

Unskilled, untrained, regular people. For the first time ever, she had the upper hand.

"Hi—YA!"

With a bit more relish than was required she flipped a farmer who was trying to strangle her over her shoulder, using his momentum to effectively topple two more.

Don't get cocky.

Most of the time it was Dylan's voice echoing in her head, but sometimes it was the others.

Cassiel—showing her how to incapacitate two people at once. Tanya—showing her how to get out of a chokehold when someone grabbed her from behind. Even Rose—teaching her a vaulted handspring that would knock down her attacker regardless of their size.

And then, all at once... things slowed to a stop.

The queen froze where she stood, panting quietly, staring out at the thirty or so people who had gathered in the street. Some of them she'd fought before, as they were already bruised and bloody. Some of them had only just arrived. Some of them had already started circling behind her.

Dylan's final lesson echoed through her mind.

And what happens when you're outnumbered, princess? What do you do?

His quiet voice steadied her as she positioned her feet on the ground.

You run.

In a flash she took off her shoe, threw it as hard as she could, then took off running in the opposite direction. A stroke of genius, she'd thought. A distraction to let her get away.

Except that when she glanced back, all thirty people were still staring right at her.

How do I run? WHERE do I run? They'll only follow!

Of course she hadn't expected a real answer, but she was still strangely let down by the silence in her own head. She had been thrilled with her success, but she wasn't delusional enough to think that she could keep it up for much longer. Eventually, one way or another someone was going to hit her. Just one good punch and she'd be down on the street.

And what were all those people going to do then?

Her remaining shoe slipped a little as she slowly backed towards the line of shops. Wondering if any of the doors were open. Wondering if the doors would hold if she managed to make it inside.

There was a subtle shift in the air. A feeling of anticipation. A squat man with a mustache standing nearest to her curled back his lips with a menacing smile.

It's now or never. You're going to have to—

The crowd surged forward.

RUN!

She didn't look to see where she was going, and she didn't glance back to see if any of them had followed. There was no need. She knew they had followed. Every single one of them. Her only hope now was to get into one of the shops.

With a surge of adrenaline she ducked into the first one she could reach, sliding to a stop on the wet stone as a barrage of different smells assaulted her nose.

What the—?!

It was an apothecary, she realized. The shelves were lined with little glass jars, each claiming to contain some sort of magical remedy, and strands of dried herbs hung from the ceiling. There was a fire still crackling happily in the hearth and a pair of mugs was steaming in the center of the kitchen table. It was then Katerina realized something very important.

She might have made it inside. But that didn't mean she was alone.

With a silent gasp, she dropped to the floor just as three people stumbled down the wooden stairs. They had the same glassy-eyed look as the rest of them, but judging by the state of their clothing they had yet to go outside. It made them calmer somehow. More predictable.

Of course, that's going to change the second they see me.

With wide eyes, Katerina watched their feet as they got closer—silently scooting around the table on her hands and knees. There wasn't a sound between them, and the young queen found herself holding her breath. Mirroring each movement carefully. Keeping just barely out of sight.

"There are people outside," one of them murmured suddenly. The queen froze in place, watching them with silent, terrified eyes. "Lots of people."

Even as he spoke, the ends of his sentences began to slur. A faint dilation came over his eyes, and by the time he finished talking Katerina was sure he couldn't talk anymore.

There was a woman standing beside him. They wore matching rings.

"We should—"

A strange shudder passed over the woman, the same shudder that rattled the shawls of the old woman standing by her side. When she opened her mouth to speak again, she was no longer able.

The smells of the shop were almost overwhelming. So many different herbs and spices, Katerina didn't know how they could stand it. The fire made everything that much worse. Heating the aroma and mixing it with a thick layer of smoke. One that was creeping up her nostrils.

The villagers were starting to press against the windows of the shop. The people inside didn't know why, but they were eager to join them. The man was about to open the door—

"Achoo!"

Nice job, princess. The queen clapped her hands over her mouth. officially demoting herself in her mind. The guiding voice in her head disowned her as the three people whirled back around.

And I'm finished.

There was only one way in or out of the apothecary, and the entire village was waiting outside. By the time she finished dispatching the three civilians—if she was even able—they would no doubt have pushed their way inside. At which point she would meet a truly unimaginable death.

They were searching for her now. Minds blunted, but eyes sharp. Cocking their heads to the side as they tried to peer around the table. The man was already licking his teeth.

Use your fire!

The impulse was almost inescapable. Already, the tips of her fingers were beginning to glow.

Use your fire and get the heck out of here!

Except she couldn't use her fire without killing a lot of people. And the only way she was getting out of there was if she massacred half the town. And that... she wasn't willing to do.

Her hands paled back to their usual color and started to tremble. Their boots had started to round the corner. With a shaky breath, she closed her eyes and forced herself to think of something better. A beautiful face flitted in and out of her mind.

CRASH!

Her eyes snapped open with a start. It was so loud! What could have—

CRASH!

There it was again! An ominous rumbling, followed by the sound of splintering wood and shattered glass. A second later there was an unmistakable cry of pain.

Katerina's heart seized up. The villagers didn't scream. Not matter how many times they got hit, no matter what happened to them, it was like they couldn't feel it. Which meant only thing.

That agonized voice belonged to someone she knew.

The three people inside the store turned, and for a minute Katerina wondered if the scream had been for her. Some gallant attempt at a diversion. Kailas and Cassiel had run this way. Then there was a final crash and villagers began to drift away to investigate. The apothecaries joined them.

Katerina uncurled her body, then slowly got to her feet.

She was completely alone. Not a single person had stayed behind. The coast was clear if she wanted to try to run, and yet one of her friends was clearly in trouble. You didn't scream like that unless... Actually, she had *never* heard someone scream like that.

I have to go help them. They'd do the same for me.

With a look of steely determination, she set her jaw and cautiously ventured to the door of the shop. It was hanging open; one of the villagers must have already been on their way inside. Through the crack, she could just barely make out the swarm of people headed across the street.

It wouldn't be easy to get there first. She'd have to circle around the back of the tavern, hope she didn't run into any people along the way, and climb through a window on the opposite side.

Okay, you can do that. Just break it into pieces. First things—

She jerked back as someone caught the hood of her cloak. At the same time, a strong hand clamped over her mouth. She tried to fight it. Tried foolishly to scream.

Then she spun around to see a pair of smiling faces.

"You guys!"

Kailas. Cassiel.

Never had she been so happy to see familiar faces. They looked like they'd been dragged backwards through a warzone, but they were still standing. Well, Cassiel was. Kailas was leaning on the fae heavily, and one side of his body seemed to have been dipped in blood.

They both looked equally glad to see her, even though the fae was shaking his head.

"Endlessly predictable; she was actually going out to save us." He shot the prince a sideways glance. "You owe me dinner rations for a month."

Katerina couldn't stop smiling, even though part of her sensed it was at her own expense. "What?"

Kailas rolled his eyes, though he kept an arm wrapped tightly around the fae's neck. "Cassiel bet that, if you knew we were in trouble, you'd try to save us."

The fae shook his head, fixing her with those beautiful eyes. "I swear I'll stamp that instinct out of you one of these days..."

Katerina looked back and forth between them, reaching without thinking to grab hold of their sleeves. She was still smiling, when the words suddenly clicked. She turned to Kailas.

"You thought that I wouldn't?"

"I *hoped* you wouldn't," he clarified, shifting his weight painfully. "I hoped you'd take the opportunity to run somewhere safe. I also thought you might have recognized the scream was mine."

Again, the words clicked. Her eyes screwed up in dismay.

"And because it was *you*, you thought that I wouldn't... wait—that was *you*?!" Her eyes widened frightfully as she looked him up and down. "What the heck happened to you?"

Her brother stared down at the floor, while Cassiel rolled his eyes.

"The idiot dropped a house on top of himself, trying to keep you alive."

Katerina blinked, then repeated it back very slowly. "You dropped a house on yourself?"

Kailas blushed, wishing very much he didn't need the fae's assistance to stand. "It sounds a lot worse than it was..."

Her mouth fell open in shock. "What the heck does that—"

"TO THE BOAT!"

The gang fell instantly silent, turning to the window.

For the first time in what felt like ages, Katerina's heart jumped in her chest. It was Dylan. It was definitely Dylan. So Dylan was definitely alive. There was only one problem.

"What is he doing?" Kailas murmured, watching as the villagers began to drift in the direction of the noise. "He can't fight off that many people at once."

Cassiel's face was grim as he stared intently out the window. "It means he can't get in here to help us. It means he's counting on us to get to the water first."

"But we can't do that," Katerina said in dismay, staring at the back of the horde. "There's only one way to get—"

"*Sera!*"

In a flash, Cassiel was sprinting across the street—dropping the wounded prince where he stood. He didn't care who was watching him, or how many villagers started to turn. His dark eyes were fixed only on his sister. And the terrifying man dragging her down the road.

Katerina let out a gasp as Kailas grabbed on to the window with a death grip.

The lovely fae wasn't moving. Her eyes were closed and trickles of blood were streaming through her ivory hair. Her body lurched through the gravel, one arm trailing behind while the other was in the hand of the biggest, meanest, most intimidating man Katerina had ever seen.

Seven feet tall. Thick, bulging muscles. And a blood-stained sneer. He dragged his prize right through the center of the road, silently daring anyone to take her away.

Of course, he hadn't counted on her suicidal older brother.

"I will tear you to pieces!"

Cassiel was moving so quickly, so blinded by rage, that he didn't notice several little things that should have told him something was off.

The way the burly man looked up in surprise the second he saw him, a grotesque smile lighting his face. The way that smile morphed into a look of cartoonish horror as the fae continued streaking towards them. The way the man started shaking a discreet hand back and forth, while Serafina herself peeked open an eye and mouthed 'go away.'

Nothing was getting through.

The fae had no weapon, but he was clearly planning on using his bare hands. He closed the distance between them, still raging in his native tongue, a promise of certain death in his eyes, when the man caught him by the back of the cloak and kissed him right on the lips.

Cassiel froze. All thoughts of homicide put on hold.

Seven hells.

"It's *me*, you idiot!"

The villagers gathered around them in a circle. Serafina smacked her palm to her face, while her older brother gazed in utter disbelief at the man holding her hostage.

"...Tanya?"

There was a shimmer of air as the shape-shifter turned back, looking as angry as Katerina had ever seen her. "Of course it's Tanya! What—you can't recognize your own girlfriend?!" A hungry-looking baker reached for her and she snapped his wrist with a backwards kick. "I want to thank you, by the way, for ruining my brilliant plan!"

"I didn't—"

"Behind you!"

Serafina jumped to her feet and the three of them started battling the people swarming their way. Kailas and Katerina looked at each other for only a moment before racing out to help.

"You made some really weird friends, Katy." Kailas shook his head.

"Yeah..." She wrapped his arm around her neck. "There's no explaining them."

The second she and Kailas got there, it became obvious what the men's method of survival had been. Cassiel took hold of the prince once more, fending off attackers, while Kailas sprayed a wide arc of fire from his hands. Not hitting anybody, but keeping them away.

"Won't they walk through it?" Katerina worried, adding her own flames to the mix.

His dark eyes danced with the reflection, burning bright against his pale skin. "They haven't tried it yet. And it won't last for more than a few minutes. Hopefully just long enough to get away."

It was a dangerous bit of work, but in a surprisingly short amount of time they had cleared a path all the way down to the river. Dylan and Aidan were waiting. Along with a stolen boat.

"Kat!"

The ranger lit up the second he saw her, straining against the vampire's supportive hand. For his part, Aidan looked equally glad to see her—though he didn't look surprised.

"I told you," he murmured, grinning at the ranger's enthusiasm. "I told you she was alive."

"Let me go, you freakin' parasite!"

The grin faded, and with a look of supreme unconcern Aidan dropped him where he stood, pretending not to see or care when Dylan collapsed against the railing of the ship. Katerina was in his arms a second later, smiling like her face might burst.

"I was so scared," he whispered, gripping her painfully tight. "When I saw you go off on your own, I thought—"

"I did what you told me," she blurted suddenly, staring up into his eyes. "All my training, all your lessons... I did what you said. I fought them off."

She'd never forget the sight of him. Bloody and beaming with pride.

Then the ship lurched beneath them and both quickly pushed to their feet.

Aidan was on the shore, pushing at the wooden hull with his bare hands. A rare tension furrowed his handsome brow as the muscles in his arms strained and shook. Cassiel was pushing right beside him, pulling in shallow breaths as his feet dug farther and farther into the sand.

The villagers had escaped the fire and were making their way down to the shore. A terrifying hum of excitement rose up among them as their eyes zeroed in on the vampire and the fae.

"Do we have any weapons?" Katerina cried in dismay. "Something we can fire down?"

"Don't worry about it."

Dylan slid back down with a careless smile. The second the others had joined him on board, every trouble or concern had somehow vanished from the ranger's mind.

"Don't worry?" Katerina stared down at him in shock. "Dylan, the whole village—"

"Cass will take care of it."

He patted the floor beside him with a contended sigh, looking highly relieved the entire ordeal was behind him. Just over his shoulder Cassiel and Aidan were trying desperately to perform the impossible, their entire bodies angling into the ship.

"Have you lost your—"

"So you remembered my lessons, huh?" He gazed up at her, those enchanting eyes glowing with sheer adoration. "Any highlights?"

The ship lurched forward another inch. Then another inch more.

"I'm telling you," he preempted when she opened her mouth to protest again, "Cass has it covered." He patted the deck again with a little smile. "It's in the bag."

When she didn't sit down, he gave up and promptly started napping. She stared in shock for another moment before clutching the railing with the others, shouting words of support.

To say it was a close call didn't show a proper appreciation for the height of the danger or the impossibility of the task. By the time the boat slid into open water, the entire cannibalistic horde had just reached the river's edge. One of them actually yanked off Aidan's cloak as he and Cassiel leapt onto the side of the ship and painstakingly pulled themselves over the side.

They spilled onto the deck in sheer exhaustion, panting and closing their eyes. It wasn't for a few seconds that they noticed Dylan, propped up and dreaming against the side.

"Is he asleep?" Aidan asked in astonishment.

Cassiel shook his head. "...*unbelievable*." With a bit of a stretch, he kicked the ranger in the leg. "Oi—princess! The ship's underway, no thanks to you. The vampire and I saved your life."

Katerina bit back a smile. It was the first time someone else had gotten called 'princess' in that particular tone. She was more than happy to share.

Dylan flashed a smile without ever opening his eyes. "You're a gem."

"You're an *a*—"

"Wake me when we get to port."

The fae dropped back onto the deck with a chuckle. The river was wide and the current was carrying them right where they wanted to go.

For at least a moment, they could take a page from the ranger's book and catch their breath. For at least a moment, they were safe.

If only for a little while.

IT TOOK SIX HOURS FOR the peaceful little river to spill out into the sea. A full moon shone bright in the sky and the stars were glowing, when they crashed the little boat into an open dock.

The whole gang winced and turned to Cassiel at the same time. The fae merely shrugged then jumped over the side. "I told you I didn't know how to sail."

The others rolled their eyes and carefully followed him.

In a fortunate turn of events they were able to find a ship willing to leave that very night, and in an even more fortunate turn of events they were able to pay for it. Fate had a way of working those kinds of things out. In this case, they merely sold the craft they sailed in on. The harbor master was delighted. They ended up with more gold than they'd need.

Less than an hour after they'd made port, they were leaving it again. Stocked with at least a month's provisions and a new pair of boots for Katerina. Sitting together on the deck as they sailed off into the open sea.

Katerina wrapped a blanket tighter around her shoulders, nestling back in Dylan's arms as she stared out at the moonlit waves.

She'd never been on a ship before. She'd never even been to the ocean. All her life she'd lived only an hour away, but her father had never permitted her to go. It wasn't safe, he'd said.

Like the castle had turned out to be any safer.

"What?" she asked quietly, unable to ignore her brother's gaze any longer. "Why are you looking at me like that?"

The rest of the friends were fast asleep. They'd been given quarters below deck, but there was something incredibly calming about the open air. The crew gave them as much space as they wanted, quietly tending the sails as they huddled together on the bow of the ship.

The Damaris twins were the only two left awake.

Kailas lowered his eyes quickly, hiding his face. Serafina was wrapped in his arms just as she was wrapped in Dylan's—the fae's white hair spilling over his chest. "It's nothing."

Katerina cast a quick glance at the sleeping ranger, then leaned closer, catching her brother's sleeve. "What? Tell me."

He paused for a moment, then hesitantly met her gaze. "I saw you fighting out there."

She stiffened, warily staring back at him. They hadn't had the same upbringing, she and her twin. In the beginning, they'd been treated as equals. But there came a point, she wasn't sure exactly when, that she'd been given embroidery while he'd been handed a sword.

Kailas was an incredible fighter. She was not.

"So?" she mumbled, suddenly sorry she'd even asked. "Not everyone's had years of lessons with a private—"

"I couldn't believe it."

She lifted her head to find him staring at her with the most peculiar expression. Something she'd never seen before. He almost looked...proud.

"When you came back to the castle, you weren't the same as when you left. You really went through a lot out there." He hesitated, editing himself. "*I* put you through a lot."

She sucked in a quick breath, then looked down at her hands. Waves of conflicting emotion swept through her, but when she lifted her head she was quiet and sure. "Alwyn put me through a lot. Put both of us through a lot."

Kailas was quiet a moment, then suddenly lifted his head. "I knew you would come."

She gave him a questioning glance, which he returned with a small smile.

"When Cassiel and I were betting before. I told him you wouldn't, but I knew you would. It's who you are. It's who you've always been."

Their eyes met in the darkness.

"You're going to make a great queen, Katy."

A thrill of warmth flooded through her, flushing her skin despite the cold. There were so many ways she wanted to answer. So many things she wanted to say.

"If we live that long."

He tossed back his hair with a chuckle, gazing out at the open sea. "Yeah... if we live that long."

With that, brother and sister shared a quick smile then drifted off to sleep. Safe in the circle of their friends. Safe in the knowledge that, for the moment, they were staying one step ahead.

They didn't notice when the captain changed direction. They didn't see the shadow of the moon drift sharply over the sail. They didn't even hear the splash when a man jumped over the side.

THE END
... well, till the next one.

Foretelling

The Queen's Alpha Series

Eternal

Everlasting

Unceasing

Evermore

Forever

Boundless

Prophecy

Protected

Foretelling

Revelation

Betrayal

Resolved

Find W.J. May

Website:

http://www.wanitamay.yolasite.com

Facebook:

https://www.facebook.com/pages/Author-WJ-May-FAN-PAGE/141170442608149

Newsletter:

SIGN UP FOR W.J. May's Newsletter to find out about new releases, updates, cover reveals and even freebies!

http://eepurl.com/97aYf

More books by W.J. May

The Chronicles of Kerrigan

BOOK I - *Rae of Hope* is **FREE!**

Book Trailer:

http://www.youtube.com/watch?v=gILAwXxx8MU

Book II - *Dark Nebula*

Book Trailer:

http://www.youtube.com/watch?v=Ca24STi_bFM

Book III - *House of Cards*

Book IV - *Royal Tea*

Book V - *Under Fire*

Book VI - *End in Sight*

Book VII – *Hidden Darkness*

Book VIII – *Twisted Together*

Book IX – *Mark of Fate*

Book X – *Strength & Power*

Book XI – *Last One Standing*

BOOK XII – *Rae of Light*

PREQUEL –
Christmas Before the Magic
Question the Darkness
Into the Darkness
Fight the Darkness
Alone the Darkness
Lost the Darkness

SEQUEL –
>Matter of Time
>Time Piece
>Second Chance
>Glitch in Time
>Our Time
>Precious Time

Hidden Secrets Saga:
Download Seventh Mark part 1 For FREE
Book Trailer:
http://www.youtube.com/watch?v=Y-_yVYC1gyo

Like most teenagers, Rouge is trying to figure out who she is and what she wants to be. With little knowledge about her past, she has questions but has never tried to find the answers. Everything changes when she befriends a strangely intoxicating family. Siblings Grace and Michael, appear to have secrets which seem connected to Rouge. Her hunch is confirmed when a horrible incident occurs at an outdoor party. Rouge may be the only one who can find the answer.

An ancient journal, a Sioghra necklace and a special mark force life-altering decisions for a girl who grew up unprepared to fight for her life or others.

All secrets have a cost and Rouge's determination to find the truth can only lead to trouble...or something even more sinister.

RADIUM HALOS - THE SENSELESS SERIES
Book 1 is FREE

Everyone needs to be a hero at one point in their life.

The small town of Elliot Lake will never be the same again.

Caught in a sudden thunderstorm, Zoe, a high school senior from Elliot Lake, and five of her friends take shelter in an abandoned uranium mine. Over the next few days, Zoe's hearing sharpens drastically, beyond what any normal human being can detect. She tells her friends, only to learn that four others have an increased sense as well. Only Kieran, the new boy from Scotland, isn't affected.

Fashioning themselves into superheroes, the group tries to stop the strange occurrences happening in their little town. Muggings, break-ins, disappearances, and murder begin to hit too close to home. It leads the team to think someone knows about their secret - someone who wants them all dead.

An incredulous group of heroes. A traitor in the midst. Some dreams are written in blood.

Courage Runs Red
The Blood Red Series
Book 1 is FREE

WHAT IF COURAGE WAS your only option?

When Kallie lands a college interview with the city's new hot-shot police officer, she has no idea everything in her life is about to change. The detective is young, handsome and seems to have an unnatural ability to stop the increasing local crime rate. Detective Liam's particular interest in Kallie sends her heart and head stumbling over each other.

When a raging blood feud between vampires spills into her home, Kallie gets caught in the middle. Torn between love and family loyalty she must find the courage to fight what she fears the most and possibly risk everything, even if it means dying for those she loves.

Daughter of Darkness - Victoria
Only Death Could Stop Her Now
The Daughters of Darkness is a series of female heroines who may or
may not know each other, but all have the same father, Vlad Montour.
Victoria is a Hunter Vampire

Don't miss out!

Visit the website below and you can sign up to receive emails whenever W.J. May publishes a new book. There's no charge and no obligation.

https://books2read.com/r/B-A-SSF-SEXU

BOOKS 2 READ

Connecting independent readers to independent writers.

Also by W.J. May

Bit-Lit Series
Lost Vampire
Cost of Blood
Price of Death

Blood Red Series
Courage Runs Red
The Night Watch
Marked by Courage
Forever Night

Daughters of Darkness: Victoria's Journey
Victoria
Huntress
Coveted (A Vampire & Paranormal Romance)
Twisted
Daughter of Darkness - Victoria - Box Set

Hidden Secrets Saga
Seventh Mark - Part 1
Seventh Mark - Part 2
Marked By Destiny
Compelled
Fate's Intervention
Chosen Three
The Hidden Secrets Saga: The Complete Series

Kerrigan Chronicles
Stopping Time
A Passage of Time
Ticking Clock

Mending Magic Series
Lost Souls

Paranormal Huntress Series
Never Look Back
Coven Master
Alpha's Permission
Blood Bonding
Oracle of Nightmares
Shadows in the Night
Paranormal Huntress BOX SET #1-3

Christmas Before the Magic
Question the Darkness
Into the Darkness
Fight the Darkness
Alone in the Darkness
Lost in Darkness
The Chronicles of Kerrigan Prequel Series Books #1-3

The Chronicles of Kerrigan Sequel
A Matter of Time
Time Piece
Second Chance
Glitch in Time
Our Time
Precious Time

The Hidden Secrets Saga
Seventh Mark (part 1 & 2)

The Queen's Alpha Series
Eternal
Everlasting
Unceasing
Evermore
Forever
Boundless
Prophecy
Protected

The Senseless Series
Radium Halos
Radium Halos - Part 2
Nonsense

Standalone
Shadow of Doubt (Part 1 & 2)
Five Shades of Fantasy
Shadow of Doubt - Part 1
Shadow of Doubt - Part 2
Four and a Half Shades of Fantasy
Dream Fighter
What Creeps in the Night
Forest of the Forbidden
Arcane Forest: A Fantasy Anthology
The First Fantasy Box Set

Watch for more at https://www.facebook.com/USA-TODAY-Best-seller-WJ-May-Author-141170442608149/.

USA TODAY
BESTSELLING AUTHOR
W.J. MAY
bring fantasy to life...

About the Author

About W.J. MayWelcome to USA TODAY BESTSELLING author W.J. May's Page!

SIGN UP for W.J. May's Newsletter to find out about new releases, updates, cover reveals and even freebies!
http://eepurl.com/97aYf

http://www.facebook.com/pages/Author-WJ-May-FAN-PAGE/141170442608149?ref=hl
and
http://www.wanitamay.yolasite.com/

Please feel free to connect with me and share your comments. I love connecting with my readers.

W.J. May grew up in the fruit belt of Ontario. Crazy-happy childhood, she always has had a vivid imagination and loads of energy.

After her father passed away in 2008, from a six-year battle with cancer (which she still believes he won the fight against), she began to write again. A passion she'd loved for years, but realized life was too short to keep putting it off.

She is a writer of Young Adult, Fantasy Fiction and where ever else her little muses take her.

Read more at https://www.facebook.com/USA-TODAY-Bestseller-WJ-May-Author-141170442608149/.